D0915392

Period

Also by Dennis Cooper

Closer
Frisk
Try
Guide
Period

Wrong (Stories)
The Dream Police: Selected Poems 1969–1993
All Ears (Journalism)

Jerk (with Nayland Blake)
Horror Hospital Unplugged (with Keith Mayerson)

Period

DENNIS COOPER

Grove Press
New York

The epigraph is from Maurice Blanchot's *The Writing of the Disaster*, translated by Ann Smock (University of Nebraska Press, 1986).

Parts of *Period* have appeared in *GOTHIC: Transmutations of Horror in Late Twentieth Century Art*, edited by Christoph Grunenberg (The MIT Press, 1997) and *Weird Little Boy*, a CD/book collaboration with John Zorn, Nayland Blake, Casey McKinney, Chris Cochrane, and Mike Patton (Avant Records, 1997).

I'm very grateful to Ira Silverberg, Amy Hundley, Morgan Entrekin, Joel Westendorf, Amy Gerstler, Marvin Taylor, Terminator, Linda Roberts, and Casey McKinney.

Published simultaneously in Canada
Printed in the United States of America

FIRST EDITION

Library of Congress Cataloging-in-Publication Data

Cooper, Dennis, 1953–
Period / Dennis Cooper. — 1st ed.
p. cm.
ISBN 0-8021-1656-6
I. Title.
PS3553.O582P47   2000
813'.54—dc21   99-42765
CIP

Design by Laura Hammond Hough

Grove Press
841 Broadway
New York, NY 10003

00 01 02 03   10 9 8 7 6 5 4 3 2 1

for Vincent Fecteau

Table of Contents

Keep watch over absent meaning.
    —*Maurice Blanchot*

Period

Chapter

A little town made up of rickety shacks largely hidden away
in some humongous oak trees that this thick fog enclosed almost all day sometimes so most residents stayed at home
though a handful might walk up the dirt road each morning
and buy some supplies while this strange deaf-mute teenager
sat on the steps of the general store writing things in his notebook and glanced around worriedly every once in a while
with this scrawl in his eyes thinking who knows what circui-
tous shit.

Nate's eyelids shut, bunched, quivered a fraction, then opened
to show off a mind built of weird contradictions. His eyes were
amber, a bit dilated, and sparkly. Too excitable to know, yeah?
So Leon checked how he was reflecting in them, and, sure
enough, he looked scared. "I got this idea," Nate said.

    "Oh?" Leon couldn't believe he was sitting around in the
presence of someone so . . . mentally out there. Hopefully,
Nate felt vice versa for him.

Nate turned away, spat. "I'm thinking we could ask Satan for something." All this bullshit was said in a thick Southern accent that made him impossible to know very well, if at all. Hence, the charisma.

"Yeah, like what?" Leon's bewilderment did something odd to his voice. Luckily, Nate was always so into his own crazy thoughts. It made others feel useless. Hence, the charisma.

"I'm thinking for sex." Nate snickered just so. There couldn't have been a more perilous moment. In the background, his boombox was playing the newest cassette by The Omen, a crappy Satanic rock band that he loved.

"You got someone in mind?" Leon said, utilizing a half-joking, fake, noncommittal, weak voice that exactly reflected his actual feeling.

"Well . . . " Nate studied Leon, his eyes growing more colorful if sort of uglier. Less distant, but much, much more fascist. In other words, incomprehensible. Maybe Nate's huge IQ was the problem. "I'll show you."

3:07: Don't like those boys.
3:09: They're evil.
3:10: Excuse me.
3:10: Reading their lips.
3:12: They got something bad in their minds.
3:13: Think it's sex.
3:13: Think they said me.
3:15: Me for sure.

3:16: Scared.

3:18: Go away.

3:20: Think of something else.

3:21: When the wind hits a treetop, it's born.

3:23: It keeps changing.

3:23: Big dog head.

3:24: Ocean wave.

3:24: Can't decide.

3:25: They're still there.

3:25: Help.

3:26: Gonna stare 'em down.

3:28: Staring.

3:29: Bored.

— Him.

— Who?

— Sitting there. Writing in that notebook.

— The guy who looks weirdly like you.

— Yeah. Let's just say theoretically . . . we ask Satan to give him to you for your sexual purposes. You know, to sort of distract you from me.

— Fuck you.

— That way you can do it with him, and we can just be best friends, 'cos—

— Fuck off.

— . . . seriously, Leon, for the million billionth time, I'm way too fucked up. Trust me.

— You say that now.

— I'll say that in Hell.

— But it wouldn't be the same with him. Come on.

— Sure, it will. He can't talk, he can't hear. It'll be like you're playing with me. You can fool around with him or whatever you want.

— I don't know.

— Look at him. He looks sort of like me if I was nervous.

— Yeah, okay. It's spooky.

— It's fate.

— Maybe. What's the plan?

— Oh, no plan yet. I'm just talking.

Leon unfocused his eyes on the swaying around of a tree outside the shack's dusty window. Its limbs were entrancingly lighted. But he couldn't connect how he felt with its beauty. So he turned his head slightly and studied a framed photograph of his only friend, Nate, in particular two amber eyes. They were a little too friendly, but nowhere near cozy enough. Finally he closed his own eyes and very neatly unlit everything in his mind 'til there was only the heat of the day—which was slow and very weighty with moisture, and laced like a shoe with the whirring of flies—and the bed, which was cold and uneven and had no effect. Thus he was left to himself. And to his imagination. And to the sizzly sun. And to the sounds of the jiggling tree. And he pictured that deaf boy's face, made a fist, closed it around himself, raised it up, then brought it down hard in the direction of Hell, up and down, over and over, until he'd completely erased shit.

Don't be scared, Nate yelled through his chapped, smelly hands. It's me, Bob. He was standing before an old shack where this outsider artist of no repute lived, worked, and sort of kept to himself. Sometimes Nate hiked way out here, and let the psychotic guy screw him for kicks.

The slat door swung open so roughly it knocked loose a yellowish dust cloud from somewhere. Out piled this grizzled type, scrubbing his paint-spattered hands with a gross rag. Obviously it's you, Bob said. He squinted hard at the woods' disheveled edge, then made a grab for Nate's ass.

Bob couldn't be around Nate without half seeing George, some dead boyfriend. He'd left this heaviness in Bob's mind. These days, Bob did whatever bullshit it took to actualize the guy's feel, from screwing near look-alikes to illustrating the past with his art like a ramshackle Disney.

Wait, Nate said. Before I forget. I want to see that new thing you're making up in the hills. Word around town was the guy had gone totally evil or nuts, on account of how freakish it looked next to everything else. Then Nate clenched his ass into a rock, and held it tight, 'til Bob promised.

9:02: Leaf shaking, tree to the right.
9:08: Bored.

9:10: Something on the road?

9:13: Nothing.

9:47: Was asleep for a while.

10:12: Deer on the hill.

10:13: Thinking of shooting that deer.

10:15: Nailed it.

10:17: It's shaking a little.

10:23: Still now.

10:31: Bored.

10:34: Okay, okay. More deer. I see 'em.

10:35: Two of 'em. Shit.

10:38: Deciding.

10:39: Aim.

10:40: Got one of 'em. Head, I think. Other deer took off.

10:43: Going down there to look.

11:12: Back. It's dead.

11:13: Want to drag it up here.

11:42: Too tired.

11:50: Nothing on the road.

11:52: Still nothing.

11:59: Bored.

12:11: Wind blowing the deer's fur around.

1:01: Was asleep for a while.

1:04: Thinking of dragging that other dead deer over here.

1:06: Yeah. I'm off.

1:48: Laid that deer down by the first deer.

1:50: Watching 'em.

1:53: Gonna push 'em closer together.

1:55: Better.

With a jab of his elbow, Nate broke the store's window. No alarm, nothing. Leon reached through the uneven star and came back with a shitload of jewelry.

They ran until they'd reached that weird place only they recognized.

Leon was so spent, he couldn't think shit. The necklaces, watches, and pins formed a garish-ass pile in the grass. It looked for all the world like Satan's hatchet face laughing or yelling in profile, from their angle at least.

The sky was so muggy and black they could barely stand up. They'd been snorting crystal meth every hour for hours. Leon felt nothing but horny for Nate by this point. That hurt. Everything was hateful apart from how wildly he longed for the fucker.

Leon shut his eyes, reopened them, and made himself look available. He never could figure out how he did that. Except that it came maybe ninety percent from the way he was built.

Nate removed article after article of clothing until there was technical human perfection, as far as Leon was concerned. There shouldn't have been anyone in the world that important. It killed him.

— Satan, it's us. We're calling you. Shit, it's fucking cold out here.

— Wait, put on some music. Put on The Omen tape. It's in the . . .

— Found it.

— Maybe louder. Cool. Now kill the cat.

— It's fucking scratching me. Shit, shit.

— Keep stabbing it.

— Okay.

— Now put it in the circle of candles. On top of the jewelry.

— Okay. Satan we're calling you. Come into the circle of candles. We got a little gift for you.

— We love you, Satan. You're the coolest.

— Concentrate.

— I am.

— Fuck, that's him. Look at that. It's like a smudge. On the cat.

— Oh, shit.

— What?

— I think he's screwing me. Ow.

— Relax, let him. It's his thing, man. Uh . . . welcome Master of Darkness. We want to ask you for something. We want you to give Leon that deaf boy. What's his name?

— Dagger. Ow, ow.

— We want Dagger to be Leon's sex slave, so he can do what he wants. Can you do that for us?

— Ow, ow.

— Give us a sign. Wait, is that it? You see that?

— Yeah.

— The wind couldn't do that, right?

— I . . . don't think so.

That? Nate said, spotting the first foggy, tree-obscured view of an average, citified house. It sat in a completely impractical spot, several strenuous uphill, twisting, turning miles away from any road. 'Cos he'd expected a huge nude statue of that George guy at least. I mean, fuck it.

Quiet down, Bob said, and opened the front door a crack. Turns out that inside the hospitable front there was zip, inkiness. Still, thanks to the scrawny, vague inflow of daylight, Nate could guess it was all divvied up into rooms, hallways, and maybe even a staircase, all painted wild black.

It's a hellmouth, isn't it? Nate said. 'Cos there was a definite essence of Satan inside. Some sort of creepy crawly glow. It etched Nate with goose bumps, then spun off a fantasy wherein Bob, no, wait, Leon, yeah, raped him, wait, while The Omen played live, no, wait, murdered him, wait, or—

4:08: Lake. Nothing else.

4:10: One fish.

4:11: Wish someone was here.

4:12: Just shot at a bird.

4:12: Missed.

4:13: Bored.

4:16: Some boy.

4:16: Watching me.

4:16: Oh, him.

4:18: Gonna write him some shit.

4:19: Hi, how's it?

4:19: His lips said, Come back to my shack with me.

4:19: What for?

4:20: His lips said, For whatever I want.

4:21: He's taking a leak on the tree.

4:21: Back.

4:23: He likes me.
4:24: He does.
4:25: Thinking about it.
4:27: Thinking.

— So you remember that spell thing?
— Not right now. I'm thinking.
— Come on.
— Fine. It worked. Whatever.
— Yep. Yesterday afternoon.
— Good for you. You got laid.
— Yeah, but listen. So I see Dagger down by the river. Turns out he can read people's lips. So I say hey. He writes in that notebook of his that he's bored, so I tell him my folks aren't around, and we walk off together.
— Mm-hm.
— Guy can't control himself. I can see it in his eyes.
— Yeah.
— So we go in the shack, and he's looking around, writing things, and I'm doing crystal, and I'm telling him he's cute in little roundabout ways, 'cos he was. It was like being with you in some weird, friendly mood.
— Fuck you.
— So I say, you know, suck my dick. And I see him tense. He writes down that he's scared, then, boom, he starts looking real weird, and you can see Satan's taking him over, then, sure enough, he writes down that he'd really, really like to suck dick, with about ten exclamation marks.

— Bullshit.

— No. So I unzip my pants, and he does it. At first I think, Yeah, suck it, Nate. And it's cooler than shit, like you said.

— Can't we talk about this later? Seriously.

— But then this weird thing happens. I start thinking, Why am I doing this? Not like, This is dumb. More like, This boy deserves better. Or I deserve better, or both of us do. So I just kind of go with the flow after that, and the next thing I know, I'm holding him in my arms, and telling him I love him, and crying. I mean, I don't know.

— Leon.

— And now I can't stop thinking about him. I mean every fucking minute. Like right now, I'm thinking, Where is he? Is he okay? Does he like me?

— Leon, not right now, man.

— But it's scary. I think I'm in love with him. We must have fucked up the spell.

— Fine. Look, I'll fix it, okay? Just leave me alone. I need to think.

— About what?

— Nothing.

About that house, Nate said. Bob sat directly across a big, tilted wooden table eating rabbit and various crisp, greenish fluff from the garden out back. The shack's walls were covered with dusty oil paintings that easily could have been portraits of Nate, if it weren't for the eyes.

I told you, Bob said, jabbing a fork at his food. It's George's house. But as far as you're concerned, it's art. It's just a house painted black inside. Then he laid his free hand on Nate's scrunched, dog-eared crotch, and made the ruckus it took to blunt the crazy fuck's vibe. Now eat.

No, let me figure it out, Nate said. He shut his eyes, and activated every brain cell that the crystal meth hadn't combusted. When they flaked, he prayed to Satan for one clink of insight. He never showed, so Nate tried Bob's effect, which sort of gave him a great, evil thought. Hunh, wait.

— Fuck, man.
— I told you. Watch. Abracadabra.
— Shit.
— In a bucket. Exactly. Follow me, and bring Dagger. Stay close.
— No problem. Ow.
— Not that close. Just grab ahold of my t-shirt or something.
— Sorry. God, this is beyond dark.
— Yeah, do you feel that? There's something horrible in here.
— You think it's a hellmouth?
— That's totally what I think. Okay. I'll light a candle. Now, where is he? Right. See his feet?
— Barely.
— Make a circle of candles around them. I'll light the wicks as you go.
— Should I take off his blindfold?
— Fuck, yeah. In a minute. There.
— Okay, hurry up. Brr.

— Satan, we call you. We offer you the sacrifice of this boy's life. Take it and please stop fucking around with our minds.

— Shouldn't we ask for something specific?

— What do you mean?

— Well, it's a pretty great gift.

— Okay, I ask you, Satan, that in return for this offering you give me . . . okay, immortality. Live forever, no one can kill me, and that kind of stuff. What about you, Leon?

— Do I have to say it out loud? I'm kind of embarrassed.

— I don't know. I guess not.

— I'll think it. One second. Hold on. Okay, there. Shit.

— Jesus fucking Christ.

— Ow, ow.

— Do you feel that?

1:07: One of 'em's killing me.

1:08: Oh, shit.

1:09: No, other one stopped him.

1:10: One of 'em's screwing me.

1:11: That one hates me.

1:11: Dead.

1:12: No, other one woke me up.

1:14: One of 'em's taking a piss on my face.

1:14: Other one stopped him.

1:15: One of 'em's strangling me.

1:17: Scared.

1:20: Okay now.

1:23: Same one's strangling me again.

1:24: Other one loves my ass.

1:24: Other one hates it.

1:29: One's kicking my ass. One's kissing my face.

1:30: Other one's strangling me.

1:30: Just died, I think.

1:31: Dead.

1:33: Yeah.

1:33: One of 'em's hugging me anyway.

1:35: Other one hates me.

1:37: One of 'em's mad at the other.

1:38: They're fighting.

1:40: Can't see 'em.

1:45: All alone.

1:49: Bored.

When Bob got home from creating his firewood, Nate was bizarrely collapsed on the shack's wobbling porch. I'm fucked, he said weakly. He tried to sit, but, getting maybe an inch off the slats, he flopped down again, feeling more octopussy than ever. That house, he said. It's evil, and—

Shh, Bob said. He hoisted Nate over his shoulder, then stumbled inside, laying him, crack, on the big wooden table. Nate lifted arm, arm, leg, leg, so Bob could undress him. Turns out there was only a head wound too lite to be fatal, yet too reminiscent of George's to leave him alone. Sorry.

Leon, Nate said. He— Then telltale hands grabbed, halved, and squashed his ass into that girlier, screwable one that faked George's or some such. Go ahead, he mumbled.

Maybe it'll distract me. He meant from Leon, whom he'd only that very minute decided he loved. Ow.

Leon walked into the crosshatched room light of the general store and pulled out the gun. Then everything in front of him smudged. Fucking weird. Thanks to the crystal meth damage or something. Or that's how he explained the effect. Like aftershocks in the eyes. Nothing he could do about it. So he held up the gun, stuck it way out in front of him. It got totally lost in the smudge. But the clerk saw it, didn't he? Yeah, uh-huh. 'Cos loose change sort of sprayed across the countertop. Greasy coins, a few dollar bills that disintegrated like lint when he grabbed them. Wiped the loot into his knapsack, missed one stupid nickel. Noticed it lying there. Shit. Don't know why he even thought to retrieve it. But he was prying it up. Or attempting to. Greasy little thing. And it hit him. How the light had gone dead. Just like that, just as vague as that sounded. Not just gone out of the nickel. It was too fucking hard to describe. Shitty fantasies. Fucking crystal meth. Concentrate. Gone out of the venture, the love, sex, murder, Satanism, robberies, okay? Like that. So he handed his gun to the clerk, and said, Fuck it.

Leon stared at the glare, focusing on the spot where he'd last seen the sheriff's impervious face before light ate it up, and kind of sunned his eyes, opening them wide, so their pupils could suck at the light, which had obviously done what it set out to do, since he'd just confessed to loving Satan, and helping Nate murder Dagger, and beating the shit out of Nate, 'cos he no longer cared about prison and death row and that, seeing as how all that beautiful light had erased shit.

Nate lies by the road. It weaves off into the mountains out there. And it reeks. He's been here for hours, partly obscured by the brush, awaiting the right car to pass, and a nice passerby. Someone in elegant clothes, whom he can fleece. God forgive him, he's broke. The sun's creepy, a hard piece of scalding red shit that has no consciousness of its own, so Nate can't tell it anything real like, Go away. Everything should have a mind. So he could communicate with it. So he could say, Grass, get taller and cover me better. Or . . . School bus, stop here, right this second, and dump all your passengers out on the road so I can fuck, rob, or kill them. He wouldn't mind if the bus said, No way, you're too fucking lowly a jerk to waste time on. Or if the sun said, Oh go ahead and burn up, you asshole. Or if he could say to this road, Hey, can you glisten a little? 'Cos that would look so unbelievable. And it would glisten for Nate, to be nice. Then it might say, Okay, now you walk on my surface awhile. And Nate would, even if it got him arrested. 'Cos the road is so peaceful or something. Anyway, everything understanding everything. People's guns saying, No, not him, asshole, kill him. And Nate's pistol would swing itself around and do the shooting for him. And he'd just go, Well, hey, I didn't make the decision. And his gun would go, Yeah, I made the fucking decision. And what could the cops do? Melt down the gun? Well, they could. And maybe that would be sad, 'cos if the gun had a mind, Nate just might be attached to it. Shit, he can't win. There's no way the world's ever gonna be totally perfect, unless nothing and no one had minds. If everyone just kind of lay there, only moving around when the wind kicked them up, or if the rain got too hard, or if there was a flood. Natural things. Nate would lie in the grass here for days, weeks, spacing out, then some storm would move him twenty feet that way, and his world would change, and he'd get to know new blades of grass and new dirt and new flies or whatever. He wouldn't die, just change. Dry out, get wet, smell one way, smell another way. No boredom, no love, no fear, no being broke, no Leon, no . . . nothing. Maybe that's what will happen at world's end, after one of the millions of viruses sneaks in folks' bodies, and no one, no matter how total a genius, can cure them. They'll just . . . collapse where they are, and never see, feel, or do anything, and eventually everyone will lose sight of each other's existence, and just become . . . what? Lumps of nature. In Nate's case, a small, smelly thing lying out in some brush. A stupid thing drifting through history, no worse or better than trees or the bugs or his gun. Oh, he longs for that day. But until then he just loves this road.

Circled

The Chevy van's one good headlight drew a circle on Nate. He had stoned eyes, long hair, ripped blue jeans, and a t-shirt with two faded words on the chest. The Omen saw their type-face, and swerved onto the shoulder. Nate gawked, climbed in back, shared two joints with some Goth kid, and crashed on the throne of a drum kit. Then they drove into the outskirts of some foggy, minuscule town. When the buildings grew too numerous, The Omen turned down a dirt road. It dragged on and on, gradually shrunk to the size of a trail, and drew an ever more treacherous course through the woods.

9:42: Dead.
9:44: It's like nothing.
9:45: Scared to move at all.
9:47: My leg hurts.
9:48: Gonna shake it a little.
9:48: Okay.

9:53: Nothing to say.
9:59: Gonna stand up.
9:59: Can't see what I'm writing.
9:59: Excuse this.
10:01: Gonna walk some.
10:03: Fell.
10:06: Lying here.
10:10: Wood floor.
10:10: A building, I guess.
10:12: Don't understand.
10:14: It just is?
10:15: Nothing to say.
10:18: Bored.

— This fog's too thick. It's creeping me out. Not to mention
the cold. Hint, hint.
— One second. You sure you don't want a turn?
— Honestly, I have no idea what it feels like to lionize fucking
some kid.
— Maybe you don't pay the right kind of attention.
— To what, the simple pleasures?
— Look at me. I look electrified, right? That's his effect. And
look at him. Look what I'm doing to him.
— He's less cute. You made him ugly. Consequently, you feel
like you're seeing the real him, the deep, incontrovertible him.
Blah blah blah.
— Blah blah blah. Exactly. Give me a second.
— You finished?

— Wait.

— Dum di dum di dum . . .

— Okay, he's yours.

— Thanks. Hey, you. What's his name again, Duke?

— Fuck if I know. Wait. Tristen.

— Hey, Tristen. Gothic asshole. Do you believe in Satan?

— What?

— No, keep jacking off. I just need some information. Tell me, are you posing inside this deathliness, or do you honestly wish to send your soul into the Hell of our music?

— I don't—

— Are you just trendy, or are you a poem?

— Shit, I can't believe I'm with you. I love the way you guys think. It's so—

— Shh. You're not our fan right now, you're our subject. Do you want to be absorbed into our imaginations? Do you want to become something that can only be identified through our descriptive powers?

— Oh, God, sure.

— You want to shed your body and become the blackest butterfly in the world?

— Are you talking about sex?

— In other words, if you could become the hallucination that your stylistic affect sketches out—

— Yeah, whatever. I can't keep up with you guys.

— Alright, put it this way. Choose between your life and our art. Which is more important, the poetry mapped by our songs, or the slow accumulation of meaningless detail that constitutes your specific identity?

— I don't know. The former.

— Right. Hold his legs, Duke.

— Like this?

— Exactly. Have you ever been in Las Vegas? You, fuckhead.

— Yeah, last year.

— That's the only time?

— Yeah. Oh, God.

— Watch. No, keep jacking off. Watch the knife. There they go.

— Shit, fuck.

— See, look at his face now. That's the deep, deep him. And what does it say? Zilch.

— Fuck, Jesus.

— Whatever, Henry. You hit an artery.

— Charming.

— You'd better finish it.

— Right. You all set with the camera?

— Yeah, go.

— I'm losing it. That was nothing. Take a left here.

— Where the Hell are we?

— Some town. You were saying . . .

— I said I'm losing it.

— No, you're not. We've been through this.

— I'm a total self-parody.

— What are you talking about, the band or the other?

— Either one. Both. They're the same thing at this point. It's like I'm fated to act out some Gothic freak show, even when I adore what I'm doing. Or something.

— Maybe what you feel isn't the point. Certainly that's true with the band, right? Trust me, as a relative adjunct, I can say it was quite the little nightmare.

— That didn't bear any relationship to a nightmare.

— Think of it this way. How many years have we been playing the same set, more or less? Three, four? I'm a zombie, you're a zombie, but the show itself functions each night, or it must.

— Yeah.

— You're forgetting that each crowd is different, however minutely. Same thing with each murder. Sure, your tastes are incredibly narrow, so the kids look alike. But they're unique. So there are these subtle little differences.

— Okay.

— Alive, then not alive. That's a huge transition. As far as they're concerned, no one else has ever died. To them, the situation is fresh by default. You don't matter. You just have to look cold and consumed, and you do.

— That's good to know.

— Give it a day or two.

— But I used to love killing. Remember? I wouldn't be able to speak.

— It was a little more epic back then, it wasn't necessarily better.

— No, I don't believe that. You got to know the situation more thoroughly. You got to see all that emotion in their eyes, and in mine. But now I—

— I think it's more generous now. To me, I mean. It's less about the relationship between you and whoever,

and more about the relationship between whoever and his
death.
— Yeah, but that's the thing. Why keep doing it—
— Look. Hitchhiker. Your type. Three o'clock.
— . . . if I'm just—
— Look.

11:21: Been walking forever.

11:21: There's just so many rooms.

11:21: Real dark. Can't see.

11:23: It can't be this big.

11:24: No way.

11:26: Tired.

11:27: Just sat down.

11:29: Wish I brung my coat.

11:33: Bored.

11:33: Gonna walk some more.

11:35: Just walking.

11:38: Wait.

11:44: Something.

11:44: No, someone.

11:45: Yeah.

11:46: Yeah.

11:48: God?

11:48: Don't know.

11:50: Gonna run there.

11:53: Running.

— How'd you get this scar?

— How do you think? The police operated on my brain. You know that. They knew about the genocide. They programmed me to kill my friends, but it didn't work. There's this whole conspiracy with the neo-Nazis, man. You're not Jewish, are you?

— No. Duke, get his jeans off.

— Straighten your legs, asshole.

— There's a systematic conspiracy to destroy the white race. I'm part of it. They programmed me to act it out. I haven't, but it's hard. I hear these voices telling me to do things from what they implanted in me. I used to be intelligent. I used to be really smart. My nickname was Calculus. You know what I'm talking about. You know about the voices.

— Sure. Sure, we do.

— Yeah, they're in the Internet. That's where they come from. They should never have made the Internet. That's the way they control everything. I can't be near computers. That's why I live in the park. We've got to start over. The Blacks and the Jews, they're lost. The homosexuals too. I was programmed to kill them. I hate them, you know. We've got to be pure. That's the only way to stop it. But we can't stop it. They can't get into the park, though. We proved that.

— So you don't like to leave the park.

— No, I leave. I can leave. I learned how. You want to take me out of the park, go ahead.

— You're already out of the park.

— Yeah, right, that can happen, yeah. I need money, you know. I don't have any money. I've got to eat something. You're going to give me some money, right? I know I'm not intelligent, so it doesn't have to be much. Fair's fair. Fair's fair.

— Do you want to die?

— Do I want to die.

— Wouldn't you love to find some peace? To stop worrying about everything?

— Are you talking about heroin?

— I want to do it now, Duke.

— What?

— I said you seem pretty intelligent.

— Thanks, you think so? No, no, I'm not. I used to be a revolutionary.

— Get him on his hands and knees.

— You know what I'm talking about. Now I'm a reactionary.

— No, hands and knees.

— I used to do what I wanted.

— You ever been to Las Vegas?

— Fuck, no. That's where they want me to go. I only do what they tell me not to do. That's not intelligence. I'm just surviving.

— Look at that.

— Beautiful.

— I'm just holding on. Wow. Nothing happens. That's all I ask for. Because I'm not even here. This isn't me. No, no. I'm the in-between. That's what I think. I'm the in-between. Yeah. I'm cold.

— You're not cold. You're something else. It just feels like cold. Duke, give me the knife.

— No, I'm definitely cold.

— You are going down, you psychotic prick. Camera?

— All set.

— What?

— Pull off the road there. We can throw him in that swamp.

— I see it.

— Are there gators around here? Hey, what's your name. Hitchhiker. Sleepyhead. What's his name, Duke?

— Nate, I think.

— Hey, Nate.

— What? Sorry. No, I've never seen any gators. Just wolves and dogs, wild dogs sometimes.

— You alright back there?

— Yeah, I'm just tripping out. I mean he's so fucking dead. You can see he's not thinking. And that his blood's not moving.

— Well, "him"'s not the accurate term anymore. Calling that "him" just trivializes whatever that is, if you know what I mean.

— Not really.

— Okay, that looks like a guy at first, sure. But the longer you look, you realize that can't be a guy. It doesn't meet the criteria. So then what the fuck is it? Well, you remember that chunk of Mars they found in the Antarctic? It's like that. It's a crude piece of something that we can't understand. It only strikes us as a guy because that's our best point of reference. Christ, listen to me. Duke, this is exactly what I was talking about before.

— Shut up, Henry.

— It's like a gift to him or something, isn't it? It's weird. I really like it. I'm amazed.

— Yeah, whatever. Forget it. Park right here.

— This friend of mine . . . well, boyfriend and I killed someone once, but we were totally out of our league, I guess. Because he didn't look like this at all. I mean he wasn't even close.

— What do you mean league? Here, Duke, help me.

— You have to move out of the way, Nate.

— Oh, okay, sorry, yeah. It sounds kind of pretentious, but we're into Satan. Not as heavily as you guys.

— Grab his feet. That's it.

— Alright, let's just . . . You can keep talking, kid. Just follow us.

— It doesn't matter. Shit, it's cold. We did this sort of spell where I sacrificed a guy we knew to Satan in return for him making me immortal. I don't know if it worked, though. Maybe it did work. Jesus, now I don't know if I'm immortal or not.

— You never know. It's possible. Been there, done that.

— Ouch. Fuck.

— Careful. Okay, this is fine right here. On the count of three, let's throw him in. Swing him.

— Wait, you guys have made people immortal too? I mean, for real?

— Yeah, sure.

— One . . . Wait, wait. My hand's slipping. There.

— That's amazing. That's like a dream. Shit.

— Okay, one . . .

— Could you tell if I'm immortal or not? I don't mean by killing me or anything. I mean just from looking.

— Yeah, you're definitely immortal. Two . . .

— Seriously?

— We'll prove it to you. Hold on a second. Three.

1:18: Found it.

1:18: It's a mirror maybe.

1:18: Like at that carnival.

1:18: Whatchacallit.

1:19: That's me I'm seeing.

1:19: Pretty sure.

1:19: I don't move when I do.

1:20: I'm in a wheelchair.

1:20: Scared.

1:21: Calming down.

1:21: See myself in some nice bedroom.

1:23: Watching.

1:24: I look sad.

1:26: Going to try something out.

1:26: Concentrating.

1:27: Hello?

1:27: I looked around like I heard something.

1:27: Over here.

1:28: My lips said, What the fuck is going on?

1:28: Excited.

1:28: I'm moving the chair closer.
1:29: I look scared.
1:29: My lips said, I'm going crazy.

— Calm down. You're such an odd guy. Don't go conventional now.
— Fucking don't.
— Come on.
— But this is too intense. I didn't think—
— Look, you're seeing this as sex. That's the problem. Think of this as a series of sensations whose collective effect is transcendence, a transcendence through our evolved understanding of the physical. If you can do that, you won't mind this.
— Yeah?
— You're immortal. So nothing's going to happen, is it? You're going to learn so much about death, and then you'll come back to life. You said you're a fan of our music. So you must know what I mean.
— Okay. No, I mean I'm honored. I really am.
— Self-understanding. That's what this is about. It's not sex. Don't demean yourself, because we don't. We're like monks. We're like aliens, right? This is an abduction. You can't understand what we're going to do. It's beyond you, okay? Just assume that you'll obtain something few humans can. You won't understand it right away. It'll take you years to understand.
— Alright.
— You okay?
— I'm okay, yeah.

— You seem okay.

— I'm okay.

— Duke, go ahead. Cut off one of his . . . Yeah, the right . . . That's it.

— You look unusually excited, Henry. Am I wrong?

— I know, I know. It's amazing. Lose the other one.

— Maybe it's because we spent some time with him.

— No, it's something else. Hey, you. Shit, what's his name again?

— Nate, I think.

— Nate. Have you ever been to Las Vegas?

— What? Ow.

— Just answer the question.

— No. I never . . . Ow. Stop, shit.

— Shh.

— Fuck, it hurts really bad.

— Relax, Nate. Let us take you into the depths of yourself. Fuck your conscious mind. Let that crap go.

— But . . . I wish you wouldn't talk.

— Well, me too.

— Let me handle this, Henry. Look, don't worry, Nate. Talking's just the map. We're giving ourselves a map. That's all. Feel what's inside what we're saying. Feel what you do to our voices, the music you're orchestrating in us. That's all it is. Don't listen to the words. The words are just the ink that the map's printed with. Oh, shit.

— What?

— He's out.

— Hell.

— You'd better finish it.

— Right. Wake up, kid. Look. No, look down here. Open your eyes. Watch the knife. There. That's all you were. All that slop. You see that?

— He sees it.

— You understand? Wake up. Listen, do you understand?

— He understands. You're going to lose him. Finish it.

— Ready?

— One second. Ready.

— So, do you want to know why I'm bored? I mean, the specific reason?

— There's a specific reason? Damn, he's heavy.

— It's not the weight, it's the flimsiness. But there's a swamp down here somewhere. I can smell it. Careful.

— Okay, why? Ouch. Why are you bored?

— It began with a videotape. Some fan slipped it to me. At Coven 13, after our gig there last month. A compilation type dealie of short homemade porns. One angle, crappy sound. All of them starring this couple.

— Them fucking?

— Not just fucking. They were in love. It's the only time in my life that I can honestly say I saw real love in action. They had sex with an intensity you just never ever see. Look, over there. Through those trees. See that? That glimmer.

— Yeah. What ages?

— Eighteen and seventeen at first. That's what I was told. By the end, the cuter one looked . . . oh, twenty? Thing is, the semicute one never seemed to get bored. Every time they fucked, he went crazy. I guess since the cute one kept growing and cutting and dyeing his hair, the other one could pretend he was fucking a new guy each time. I can't explain the cute one's reaction.

— Which was?

— Emotional. Out of his mind grateful. Anything goes. I love you, I love you, I love you.

— I want to see that.

— I've got it at home. Anyway, there was this gap between the final two porns. Years, maybe. The cute one looked burnt. And the sex was still wacko intense, but it had this consensual, one-sided S&M vibe. You could categorize it, which was sad. Anyway, the semicute one was in the middle of fucking the cute one when, totally out of the blue, he shot himself. The cute one, I mean. Just put a pistol in his mouth, and pulled the trigger.

— Jesus.

— Yeah, huge surprise. And the semicute one lay around on the cute dead one's back for a second. Then he looked in the camera, and I swear the expression on his face was so heavy that his features couldn't handle it.

— You have to show me this.

— They couldn't translate the guy's reaction at all. I don't mean his specific features couldn't. I mean human features in general. It was beyond them. It was something really new. Something that didn't fall into the usual categories, and not a hybrid either.

— Like some kind of biological UFO?

— Well, yeah. Except UFO's too pictorial. Anyway, I can't get that face out of my mind. They'd been completely in love, I mean obviously so. And there was so much history between them. There had to be so much going on in that face.

— I'm lost.

— I want that look on my face. And this won't do it. All this shit. Or it would have already. But there was a moment when we were doing Nate here that I thought, You know, if he were immortal . . . if he could live through this . . . if I failed, basically, I might feel like that semicute guy.

— That's interesting. Shit, he's slipping. Can you take his arms for a second? Thanks.

— Hurry. You got 'em?

— Yeah. Sorry.

— Just through these bushes here.

— Okay. Well, good luck.

— With what?

— With finding some guy who's immortal.

— Oh, right. You ready?

— Yeah. On three.

— One, two . . .

2:11: What are you seeing?

2:11: My lips said, Me.

2:12: Thinking.

2:12: My lips said, I'm hearing voices now. God.

2:12: Thinking.

2:13: My lips said, I have so many problems. I hate it.

2:13: Where are you?

2:13: My lips said, My room.

2:15: I'm rolling around in that room looking scared.

2:16: My lips said, I'm just going to believe this is real or I'll go insane.

2:16: Can you see me?

2:16: My lips said, I see myself. Fuck.

2:17: It's dark here.

2:18: My lips said, What are you?

2:18: Same person as you.

2:19: My lips said, My name's George.

2:19: Don't understand now.

2:19: I look scared.

2:20: Scared.

Cavemen

See that mirror? George said. That's the way into a different dimension. I know it sounds insane, but I go there sometimes. Mentally. That's what's going on. I wanted to tell you, because I know you think I'm just stoned.

I can't believe this, Walker said. Fine. Okay, then tell me about it. I'll just sit here and listen.

Well, I'm living in two worlds. I'm here like this, and I'm somewhere else, too. In there. A place really different from here. I'm pretty sure one of them only exists in my mind, but I can't tell which one anymore. Because they're both foreign now.

Look, you really shouldn't do drugs.

No, it's not like that. I knew you were going to say that. I can make it come and go. I could open the other dimension right now if I wanted. Or I could stay here with you. I'm kind of like a god.

Go on, then. Here, I'll hold your hand, if you're worried. I want to see something.

5:28: You're there.

— Yeah. Walker, can you hear that?

— That being what?

5:28: Don't like it when you go away.

— But you don't understand what this is doing to me. I'm in the middle, and that's very confusing. I'm not like you. I'm fucked up.

— I understand.

— No, Walker, I'm talking to myself.

5:29: But you got your friend, and a nice place. It's dark here. Can't find my way out.

— Can you hear that?

5:29: He can't hear me. See that by his face.

— Hear what exactly?

— My reflection in that mirror. It's talking to me. This is what I was telling you about.

5:30: Been thinking something. You want to know what?

— I honestly don't hear a thing, George. Just you.

— I'll be quiet, and you listen very closely. Okay, go ahead and say something.

5:30: Got this idea.

— That. That voice.

— I'm sorry.

5:31: Figured out a way to be together. You and me.

— You did?

— George, maybe you should—

— Wait, shh. One second. What do you mean?

5:31: It's kind of crazy.

— You're scaring me, George. Look at me. Stop looking in the mirror for one second.

5:31: Let's both kill ourselves. At the same time.

—How?

5:32: With guns. Got mine, like I said. You told me your dad has one hidden somewhere.

— George.

— But you said you were already dead. Didn't you say that?

5:32: That's my thought. If we kill ourselves, maybe you can come here.

— Oh, God, I don't know. I can't think about this right now.

5:33: Or the opposite.

— Walker, help. Do something.

— Tell me how.

5:33: Wait.

— Hold me.

5:33: Wait.

I understand, Walker said. So, let me guess. Let's say you're sitting around in here doing whatever it is you do these days, and . . . wham, it just happens? It could happen again any second, right?

If I looked in the mirror, George said. I'm not sure, but I think it's whenever I see my reflection in something. That's why I can't look in your eyes. That's why I begged you not to bring Nate. Because he looks so much like me.

Of course he does. That's why I found him attractive. But he's no you, George. That's clear now. I tried to replace you with Nate. It's true, I did, but I can't. Or not completely. Listen.

Yeah, and every time I come back to this world, it's much scarier here. Don't you feel different? Because you seem different lately.

If anything, I'm less different, Walker said. It's strange, in fact. Lately, I've been feeling more sure of myself. What I want, what I don't want. Notably so. That's what I'm saying.

It's not just you, George said. It's Leon, too. He broke up with me for no reason at all. You never call me back. And you wrote this scary book about me. I can't believe it. It's like a horror movie.

You should never have read this. I didn't realize you would take it so literally. You do realize that's what you're doing. You know this whole mirror thing's straight from my novel. I'm sorry you read it. I am.

But you never want to hang out with me. Or make those little movies anymore. Or even talk to me. Not like you did. Don't you think that's weird?

Well, you're hard to be around. It's understandable, of course. You've changed, and you had to, but . . . Look, I feel as guilty as hell. But that's what I'm saying. I think we can reverse all this. Listen.

Here's what I think, George said. As long as I'm alive, you'll get weirder. Everyone will. It's me, I'm doing it. Not this me, the other me. The one who transmits his thoughts to me. I mean my thoughts to me. I mean the me in there. Shit.

Let me help you, Walker said. I have an idea.

Whenever I talk to myself, it changes everything here. Things about my other life seem to come back with me. Here is getting scarier than there now. I'm more and more like him, or he's more like me. That's it, yeah. But he's stronger.

So there's someone exactly like you. In that mirror. Am I right? Another you. You like you were before that awful thing happened. I'm right, aren't I?

Well, he says I'm him. That I'm a reflection of him. He says where he lives, strange things go on all the time. Magic things, evil things. I guess I'm starting to believe what he says. Because he's so confident, and I'm always confused.

Here's my idea, Walker said. You remember how things were. You know, before. I rejected you, true. I wrote this book, I know. I tried to have my cake and eat it too, or whatever they say. But I can't, obviously. Like I said.

I think this whole thing is a fantasy, George said. I'm somewhere else looking at this in a mirror. This is where I wish I could live, but I'm not strong enough to survive here. I'd go crazy. I'd kill myself.

Not necessarily. Listen. Not if we were together. That's what I'm trying to tell you. I think if we start it all over again, that'll change things. Like this. What I'm doing right now. You used to love this.

That's what I mean. You're all so different. It's getting harder to believe in this world anymore. I want to be somewhere else. Like in there, where it's simple. Where it's dark.

Then go ahead, George. Seriously. Ask your other self what he thinks you should do. How about that? I'll bet you anything he agrees.

5:51: Can't tell. You there?
— I just have to ask you a question. I'm really confused.
5:51: Don't go like that.
— I know. I'll try.
5:51: Gotta tell you something.
— Wait. First, is this okay? What he's doing to me. He says it's okay. But everyone who's ever done this stopped loving me. I think they never did. I mean love me at all.
— What does your friend in the mirror say?
5:51: Thinking.
— He's thinking, Walker.
— God, I've missed you.
— See? Listen to him. Do you see what I mean?
5:52: Thinking.
— If you're me, like you say, can't you decide what to do? Because I can't. I'll just let him do it. I will. That's how I am.
5:52: Never been loved like that. 'Cept once.
— Wait, Walker. Wait. Hold off.
5:52: Leon. That's his name.

— Leon's my boyfriend's name, too. Oh, God.

— George.

— Walker, please.

5:53: He did this.

— But . . . is it okay?

5:53: That's the one time.

— I can't . . . think.

5:54: George?

— Look at me, George.

5:54: Don't go.

5:55: Okay.

5:56: They're kissing.

5:59: Doing other things.

6:01: Watching 'em.

6:02: Excuse me.

6:03: Too excited to write.

6:03: Sorry.

6:05: Remembering things.

6:06: Got me hard.

6:06: Thinking.

6:06: George?

— Huh? What?

6:06: Think it's okay.

I'm scared, George said. I'm not supposed to feel this much
for people. You know that. The doctor said I shouldn't. Everyone says that. But now you're incredibly important to me, and
I don't . . . I can't . . .

Listen, Walker said. Shh. Okay, that was really stupid. I'm sorry. I thought it would work, but it hasn't. I'm sorry. Just forget that ever happened. Let go. Please, George. Seriously. It's too much.

Oh, God. This is what I mean. I don't belong here. I don't make sense anymore. I feel too much, and no one else feels anything. Like you. You used to say you loved me all the time. It used to be so different.

Stop it, George. I wish I were a better person. I wish none of this would have happened. I do. But you're just so fucked up. I understand, but you used to be so different. Let go.

But I was always like this. I just didn't say anything. I'm being honest now. Oh, God, don't leave. Fuck. Don't make me feel this then leave. Please, Walker. I'll kill myself. You don't know.

Crippler

The last time George phones, I'm updating his page on my website devoted to Walker Crane's *Period*, oddly enough.

"I know you're busy," he says.

"Just a second."

The George Miles Zone is nondesigned, like a high school year book. It's a square grid of thumbnails, showing "George" in several outfits, locales, and emotional states. Scrolling down, there's a link to my index-in-progress of characters, scenes, dialogue, and ideas that are supposedly spun off Crane's "friendship" with George. Or that's the rumor. Fans have posted their specs, and I've just added six of my own.

"Make Walker call me, Bob. I'm flipping out. I'm losing it. I think I'm going to kill myself." Then George breathes, and I listen to him and the gurgling computer.

"Alright," I say. "But I have to do something first."

I turn off the cellphone, write a note to myself, save the updates, close Netscape Composer, shut down my computer, switch off the modem, then walk into the living room, fishing around in a pants pocket.

EgoreG (*sic*) lies on the couch, watching Animal Planet. Long story short, he has a malignant brain tumor the size of an alarm clock. Until last week, he studied ballet at the community college. Then a stroke crashed the world, squelched his thinking, and put some new spin on subhuman behavior. It's given his storybook face the illusion of depth, and left me completely alone with his ass, which is so well built, we used to joke it was keeping him alive, like a huge white corpuscle.

"Here." I hand him what looks like his new medication, but it's not. Not by any stretch of the imagination.

— If you're just joining us, we're in The Darkness. I'm Leon. It's two minutes after midnight, and I just played a set by The Omen. If you haven't heard, they're playing Coven 13 this Friday night. Tickets at No Life, Vinyl Fetish, and Aron's. It's their only local show this year, and you definitely want to be there. Okay, I'm going to take some phone calls. Hi, we're in The Darkness.

— Yeah, hi Leon. This is Kurt. I don't know if you remember me from last week.

— Sure. How's your witching hour going?

— Yeah, that's why I called. I'm kind of freaked. My . . . my parents are in Mexico, and I'm alone here, and this weird thing just happened.

— What's that, Kurt?

— I was sitting here listening to your show, and doing something else that doesn't matter, and I saw this thing that was

kind of gray. It was hanging in the air, and then it just . . .
moved inside me, like disappeared inside me.

— Are you loaded, Kurt?

— No. I mean, yeah. I mean, just a little. I mean, I don't think
that's it.

— Okay, how do you feel now that the thing's inside you?

— I don't know. Okay, I guess. But I had this weird idea that
it could be cancer. Like that's how you get cancer. I don't
know if you saw that *X Files* where—

— Oh, sure. But that was a guy who was cancer. He was a real
person.

— Yeah, that's right. Okay. Right, that makes sense.

— Look, you're probably just . . . First, what drugs are you on?

— Just some pot. That's what I mean. I'm not really . . . you
know, high or anything.

— I'll tell you what. Stay cool, and if you start feeling weird,
call back, okay? Promise me.

— Yeah, yeah. Okay. That's cool.

— Alright, thanks, Kurt. Poor little guy. It's a strange world,
that's for sure. Okay, we've got to pay some bills here. I'll be
back in a few.

Walker saw George at Coven 13, maybe four years ago. He
was a guest at some Sony executives' VIP table. A searchlight
stalled on his face just when Walker was scanning the club
for a bar. One of Walker's best poems had been used as the
lyrics for "Paraloss," a minor hit for the Goth band Lestat. At
the time, they were recording for Macy, Sony's artsiest label.

According to the guitarist, Macy was little more than a front
for the notorious porn outfit, YMAC. Their tapes featured
drug-scrambled teen-idol types having bored, unsafe sex inside trendy scenarios. Walker guessed he was looking at Dagger, a sullen pothead who never actually got laid, in *Buff: The
Vampire Slaves II, III,* and *V.* Walker asked Lestat's drummer,
who couldn't confirm, but suggested he find the hidden *X* on
Macy's website, then changed the subject. Late that night,
Walker logged on, found it, clicked, and wound up in a cyber-
brochure wherein YMAC's teenaged stars sold their undies
and entertained offers.

ANONBOY16:   Did you find that webpage?
MINDMELD5:   I think so. It says The George Miles Zone across
the top?
ANONBOY16:   That's it. That's him.
MINDMELD5:   Let me just get an initial reading here. Think
about the subject of these pictures. Clear your mind of every-
thing else. Have you turned off the lights?
ANONBOY16:   Yeah. Okay, I'm thinking about him. But can
I ask you how this works just really quickly?
MINDMELD5:   Do you mean why do I insist on performing
my services in cyberspace?
ANONBOY16:   Yeah.
ANONBOY16:   Hello?
MINDMELD5:   Cyberspace is a mystical zone where time
doesn't exist. Binary code is an artificial form of human men-
tal energy. That's been proven. The Internet has given psychics

an enormous leg up in our practice. By simultaneously keeping in contact with you in this Instant Message format, and reading this boy's energy through these JPEGs, I can create a psychic link between all three of us that would be impossible anywhere else. If we could get this boy into a chatroom with us, that would be optimal, for my purposes. But you say you have no idea who he is.

ANONBOY16:   Just what it says about him on the webpage. But I feel like I know him. I don't want to say too much.

MINDMELD5:   We'll try to circumvent the energy of the person who made this webpage, but I don't think that will be a problem. I expect a very strong reading. Now let me concentrate, and you'll hear from me again momentarily.

ANONBOY16:   Go for it.

I stumbled on *Period*, thanks to a tip from this e-mail acquaintance. He adored the book, and recently shot himself in the head, à la the "George" character. Unlike Nidsen@aol.com, my fascination lies not in "George"'s myriad problems, per se, but in the novel's tricky, ulterior form. Thanks to the website, EgoreG, and two guests who should be arriving any minute, I'm this close to solving its puzzle.

"Can you hear me?" I say, and look into EgoreG's eyes. They're jiggling over some inky locale that I couldn't begin to imagine.

EgoreG nods, or rather the drug nods, and EgoreG's pale, grave face is moved up and down inadvertently.

"Help me out here." Then I grab one of his wrists, and

drag him into the guest room, while he lazily kicks over tables and lamps.

Long story short, *Period* is about a mysterious house, set in some sketchily rural locale. It's the work of an artist, "Bob," coincidentally. He's obsessed with a younger guy, "George," who'd killed himself years before in an identical building. "Bob" hopes that by replicating the context where "George" died, the guy might return to the world in some fashion. It's an ickily heart-tugging quest that defies nature's laws and conventional logic, but it does end up serving a purpose. Thanks to him, "George" reemerges, better than new. The only question is whether the artist's success is an example of love co-opting form, as some would have it, or the complete opposite.

The guest room is my homage to that artwork. This being reality, it's just a product of black paint, a wooden chair, a mirror I bought at IKEA, and now EgoreG, who'll pretty much nail Crane's description of "George" once my drug architects that scared look off his face.

MINDMELD5:   I believe I have the energy source. There is difficulty, however.
ANONBOY16:   What do I do now?
ANONBOY16:   Hello?
MINDMELD5:   There is a terrible negative energy here. Hold on.
ANONBOY16:   Do I ask you questions, or what?
ANONBOY16:   Hello?

MINDMELD5:   Ask your questions.

ANONBOY16:   Okay. I have so many. I guess the main one is, How can I meet George? Tell him I have to meet him. Tell him it's important that

MINDMELD5:   I'm getting interference from someone named Bob.

ANONBOY16:   he see me. It's hard to explain. Bob? I think the person who does this website is named Bob.

MINDMELD5:   Tell me what you know about Bob. I'll try to isolate his energy, and remove it from the equation.

ANONBOY16:   I don't know anything about him. He does that website. If you looked at any of the other pages, you can tell that he's kind of a strange guy.

MINDMELD5:   Who is Dagger?

ANONBOY16:   Dagger? I have no idea. Dagger. Let me think. No.

MINDMELD5:   I'm getting a very strange reading. Hold on.

True to form, Dagger sulked, maintained his distance, and buried his face in a bong. He seemed mesmerizingly studied, a cute poseur doing whatever he could to remain one-dimensional. Then Walker opened the couch bed, screwed his old Betacam onto a towering tripod, and discovered Dagger's secret. He sobbed, shook, begged for any sign of affection, then reconstituted the moment he came. Walker's poems were wordy mazes, known for obscuring their point with complex turns of phrase and eerie special effects. But deep inside, they were just goony crap about love, and Dagger's style seemed to mirror his interests. So Walker strung him along for a year, making half-assed excuses to reshoot their screen test. One night, Dagger didn't show up, or return Walker's pages for over a month. It was confusing until Walker switched on the news, and saw that impassive face, outlined in black, with the caption "George Miles."

— Hi. We're in The Darkness.
— Leon, hey. This is Roman. Uh, Roman Drake.
— No last names, please. What can I do for you?
— That's great about The Omen.
— It sure is.
— Hey, do you surf the web?
— No way. I'm much too paranoid.
— So you've never checked out this website called www. period.com? It's this weird fan site about that writer Walker Crane? I'm checking it out right now, and you're mentioned on one of the pages.
— Oh, yeah. Well, it's kind of embarrassing, but I named myself after a character in his book. So that's not me. That's the character.
— Wow, that's pretty funny. So you don't know this guy? The writer, I mean.
— Well, we have a . . . uh, friend in common.
— He's got to be pretty intense, or not? I can really relate to that book. It's just . . . Wow, I don't know. It's pretty sick stuff, you know? So . . .
— He's a complex human being.

— Does he ever go to Coven 13 or anything? I could see knowing him.

— Yeah, he does. Look, I don't know what your sexual orientation is, but . . .

— I'm gay.

— Okay. God, is this the place for this? Oh, Hell. Look, I was boyfriends with the guy he wrote that book about, okay? George Miles. I thought it would be cool, because he was the famous George and all that, but—

— Wow. Yeah, I saw those pictures of him on the website. He's a total babe. You really scored.

— I'd rather not get into that. So I don't know what to tell you. Crane is a messed up human being, okay? Not cool and evil like you'd think. I mean, he's a big influence on me, and I owe him a lot. And I should never have gotten involved with George. I mean I totally forced myself on the poor guy, so it's my own fault, but—

— So how could I meet that George? I mean, if you're over him.

— You're not listening to me. Okay, look. I'm not the person to talk to about this. A lot of people dig Crane's book. I used to, until I realized what it was really about. But whatever.

— Yeah, I'm kind of, uh . . . Wow. Like a huge fan.

— Well, thanks for sharing your thoughts.

— Does he ever go to Coven 13?

— Who?

— George Miles.

— No, he doesn't go to Coven 13. He never even leaves his room. He's not like he is in the book. Trust me, you don't want

to know. Okay, thanks, Roman. We've got to take a break.
We're in The Darkness.

I met Henry and Duke in a newsgroup, alt.books.gothic.period.
Their take on the novel was lurid at most. Still, we set up a
private chat, shared our love-hatred for George, his look-alikes,
and their asses, then met for drinks. For reasons that I will explain, they dress, coif, and make up their faces to simulate the
average parents' worst nightmare.

"So this is George in quotes," Henry says. He lifts
EgoreG's bangs, then rolls his eyes until I yank down those
sweatpants.

"Tell me you don't want to swipe him with a credit
card," I say. That line is straight out of *Period*, and I've been
dying to use it.

Henry slips a knife from some part in his leathers, and
menaces EgoreG's ass, which isn't exactly what Crane had in
mind.

"Wait a second." Duke frisks the upper half of his cos-
tume, unearths an expensive silver Nikon, gets it in focus,
takes a picture or two, then signals Henry to lower the boom.

Henry and Duke have a band, named and styled after
the fictional rock band in *Period*. "The Omen," as they're
called, are peripheral to the plot, but their music enchants
two minor characters, "Leon" and "Nate." It's an unpopu-
lar take, but I insist "George"'s comeback has nothing to do
with the quote unquote power of love meeting art, and
everything to do with "The Omen"'s effect on these boys. It's

their related collusions with Satan that cause the penultimate miracle, to simplify an elaborate plot. Anyway, that explains why I've upped the original ante and brought "The Omen"'s equivalents into my little equation.

"So, Bob. You're staying out of our way," Henry says. "Because you're not in this scene, unless I misinterpreted something."

"My thoughts exactly," I say, and take a seat on the chair. Actually, The Omen aren't in it either, but I suppose I'm in shock.

— We're in The Darkness.
— What's going on, Leon?
— Nothing much. What's going on with you?
— Not much. Can I ask you what you think about the after-death experience? Do you think it's real?
— First of all, what's your name?
— Oh, it's Bradley, sorry. I want to know about the after-death experience because my brother got killed in a car accident yesterday, and—
— Weird.
— Yeah, it's really weird. He was cool. He liked your show a lot.
— What happened?
— I don't know. He just sort of hit somebody. Head on, I guess. He drinks a lot and stuff. So . . . do you think he, like . . . do you think he's somewhere? Because I don't really believe in that shit, I mean stuff. Sorry. I mean I think he's

probably just rotting. I mean fuck it, you know? Oh shit,
sorry.

— Most people think there is something, but I don't think
anybody knows what it is. I think there's a Hell. I think Hell
is the answer to all of our stupid human questions. I think
when you die, if you're cool, you go to Hell and "merge
blacks," to quote The Omen.

— You do?

— Yeah.

— Me too. I think Tim's in Hell. So, anyway, that's cool about
The Omen playing.

— Yeah, it is.

— Are you going to be there?

— I wouldn't miss it.

— Okay, cool. Well, maybe I'll see you there.

— Yeah, if anyone wants to come up and say hi, I'll be wearing a red, longsleeved Marilyn Manson t-shirt and one of those
Peruvian skull necklaces you can buy at La Luz de Jesus.

— Cool. I'll look for you.

— Thanks, Bradley. Good luck with the thing about your
brother. We're going to take a break. We're in The Darkness.

When George was found raped, mutilated, and practically
dead in the desert, emotion savaged Walker. To fight back,
he wrote a novel that gave his poetic devices a job, to rebuild
George's ruins into the cute, inaccessible kid with the nickname. It was all very vague, since he didn't know who he was
writing about. *Period* flopped, until some band stole the name

of his fictional band, and had a moderate hit. Thanks to them, Goth kids investigated the novel, and, having few preexisting beliefs, took its intricacy as enlightenment. They set up websites and chatrooms, stole the characters' names, mistook their own problems for George's, and tracked Walker down for the cure. He fucked dozens, then focused on Nate, who bore the closest resemblance. By then, the real George had recovered, in part. He was confined to a wheelchair, addicted to painkillers, half insane, and, most complicatedly, less riveting than his look-alike.

ANONBOY16: Hello? Are you still there?

MINDMELD5: I apologize. The reading is very peculiar. Let me explain. I am reading that there are many energy sources, not just the one. This makes no sense. I have at least four distinct energies connected to these pictures. There is an energy named George Miles. There is one . . . a very powerful one . . . I can't determine its name yet. There is one . . . Egoreg? Can that be right? There is Dagger. Wait. This is strange. I am getting an unusual reading from you. You are also connected to these pictures. Is this making any sense at all?

ANONBOY16: That's so strange. Yeah, it does. I didn't want to say anything, but I have this strange feeling that those could be pictures of me. It's a long story, but

ANONBOY16: I have amnesia. The police found me wandering around in the woods, and I guess some really bad things had been done to me, but I don't remember anything. I don't even know my real name, or where I

ANONBOY16:   lived, or anything. But I saw these pictures on
the web, and I had this strong feeling about them. And they
look just like me, I think.
MINDMELD5:   What all of you are doing is tearing him apart
psychically.
ANONBOY16:   But I don't even know him. I'm not doing
anything.
MINDMELD5:   Perhaps it's something you did before. That
could be it. Wait one moment. Do you know the name Etan?
ANONBOY16:   Etan? No. But I don't know what you mean
about
MINDMELD5:   The one named Etan is the strongest energy
source.
ANONBOY16:   tearing him apart. I don't know who Etan is,
unless I'm Etan. Like I told you, I don't know who I am.
MINDMELD5:   Wait. Something is happening.

EgoreG entered my life through the website. He sent an
e-mail, claiming "George"'s ghost had come across him one
night, liked his likeness, and disappeared inside his body,
which changed his real name to that dumb anagram. He attached a self-portrait to bolster his theory. Unfortunately, it
was such a cute shot that I threw away logic, and sprung for
his airfare. But, of course, he was just photogenic, and everything else was the tumor. Or I see that now.

    Long story short, Henry has carved a crude frame
around EgoreG's ass, ripped it up, passed it sideways to Duke,
dug through some undergrowth, found a flooded compart-

ment, cleared it of organs, punched a little hole in the bottom, watched it drain, and is smashing the structure inside with a leg he just snapped off my chair.

I'm a little depressed, leaning in a corner. "Guys, hey. Listen."

"What? Shut up," Henry says, realizing it's me.

I'm studying the aforementioned mirror. In *Period*, "George" hallucinates that his reflection is someone named "Dagger." "Dagger" thrills everyone in the flat, backwards world, particularly "Bob," who may know about the more dimensional "George." It's complicated, but "George" shoots himself, which causes "Dagger" and he to change places. Or something like that. More importantly, boys in the mirror's world-ette can't be killed, which is why I'm fixated on mine. Anyway, the switcheroo doesn't work, not here, not now, not on EgoreG, at least.

"It's just that he was supposed to kill himself," I say. "That's all." I guess that's splitting hairs at this stage. But I'm tired. We're all tired.

Crane's work depends on a reader's conjecture, with one big exception. Suicide is the act that makes "George" haunt the artist, which causes to him build the house on which the narrative pivots. Without that house, there is no novel. Without the novel, this is my simple apartment. If that's true, then Henry's just killed someone who would have been dead in a month or two anyway, period.

— We're in The Darkness. Who's this?
— Leon?

— Oh, great. I'm on the air, George. Thanks a lot, Ed. Ed is the guy who screens callers for me, everybody.

— What?

— Alright, fine. Briefly, very briefly, this is my ex-boyfriend, George. Christ, the show is getting so personal tonight.

— Leon, I need to talk to you. Please.

— Why? Why in the world do you want to talk to me, George? I mean, really, why?

— I keep thinking about something, and I can't stop. I'm really losing it. I know I always say—

— God, how stoned are you? Look, George, we broke up. Do you know what I mean? You've got to sort of do something else when you get like this.

— I'm scared. I keep thinking about killing myself, and I can't stop. I tried to call Walker, but—

— That's Walker Crane, the writer we were just talking about. An evil man. He made George get completely dependent on him, and then he dumped him, and exploited him for that novel, the fucking psychopath. He used him, alright? This is what I was talking about, Roman, if you're still listening.

— What?

— George and I broke up last week. Okay, I broke up with him. He needs to go to a rehab center or a mental hospital or something, but he won't, and he makes everyone he knows fucking deal with it. Oops, sorry about that, Ed. Anyway, he's had a horrible life. I'm not saying that he hasn't. Really evil things have happened to him.

— Leon?

— What, George?

— I'm going to kill myself tonight. I'm pretty sure.

— George, I can not do this right now. Look, I swear, if you call me at home tomorrow, I promise I'll pick up, okay?

— You won't.

— Oh, great. Now you're going to make me worry about you. That's so typical. Jesus.

— Don't worry about me.

— Yeah, I wish.

— I, you know . . .

— George? Oh, great. Is he gone, Ed? He hung up. Alright, sorry about that, everybody. Let's take a break, okay? I need one. We're in The Darkness.

One night, George shot himself, just like in *Period*, and Walker's order collapsed. He hid his emotions in poems, numbed them with Nate, buried them under his fan mail, then joined his fans' escapades into the novel. But where they saw dense, hairpin mysteries spiraling into some ever backpedaling truth, he just saw machinery, designed to change someone too painful to love into something so perfect, it would transcend mere attraction. In *Period*, an artist not unlike Walker spent his life trying to recreate "George" in his art. He finally succeeded, with the support of an evil, omniscient strain in his environment. When he realized the "George" he'd made was deformed by his weak imagination, he had to kill himself, in order to satisfy the book's mirrorlike structure. In the real world, things weren't that simple deep down and complex on the surface. It was more like the opposite, meaning Walker and everyone else George Miles touched, in whatever form, could do nothing but wonder about him, and suffer the consequence.

ANONBOY16:   Hello?

ANONBOY16:   Hello?!!!

MINDMELD5:   Someone is dead. It might be the boy in the pictures, or it might be . . . Wait. No, it's not the boy in the pictures. This makes no sense to me. Everything is reconfiguring. Hold on.

ANONBOY16:   What the hell is going on? You mean dead like DEAD?

MINDMELD5:   Almost nothing is there now. Nothing where he was. I have never experienced anything like this. I've lost everything except your energy and the energy named Etan.

ANONBOY16:   I guess I don't believe you.

MINDMELD5:   I won't be able to explain this phenomenon. It is beyond my abilities. It's unique to my experience. Would you like to send a psychic message to the person named Etan? That is all I can do for you.

ANONBOY16:   Shit.

MINDMELD5:   I apologize.

ANONBOY16:   Okay. Tell him that when someone who wants to know about George Miles contacts him . . . Wait, how do I contact him?

MINDMELD5:   Hold on.

MINDMELD5:   Send him an e-mail at this address. NAtetan@aol.com. Attach a picture of you if that's possible. Do not tell

him why you're contacting him. Just send the picture, explain
that you need to talk to him, and give him a time when you
will be online. Can you do that?

ANONBOY16:   Sure.

MINDMELD5:   Hold on.

MINDMELD5:   Yes. The message is sent. I feel a positive re-
ception. The one named Etan has enclosed the energy that I
have sent to him. I feel that he will be receptive to your e-mail.
Can I do anything else for you?

ANONBOY16:   No, I guess not.

I'm in my office, showing Henry the updated website. Duke's
in the guest room, still snapping pictures, the last time I checked.
I wish they'd leave, and drive EgoreG into the desert, like we
agreed. But Henry's lost in The George Miles Zone, clicking
open and closing some JPEGs. Inexplicably, it's the page on my
website that gets the most hits per month by a gigantic margin,
even though it was sort of an afterthought.

    "I swear I know this kid," Henry says. "I can't remem-
ber from where, though."

    "George is a recluse, so I'd be surprised." That re-
minds me.

    "I'm thinking on film, TV, something." He opens a head-
shot, click-click enlarges it into a backlit abstraction, and stud-
ies his vague, pixelated reflection.

    "I don't know what to tell you," I say.

    I walk into the guest room, nod at Duke, avoid stepping
in EgoreG, and hunt around for my cellphone, which got

knocked or kicked under the busted chair, but appears to have survived, or at least the automatic dial button is glowing.

"Crane, are you there?" I ask a machine. "It's Bob. I know you said to stop hassling you, but George Miles keeps phoning. Can't you call him one time, so he'll get off my case? I'd appreciate it."

"Was that the Crane?" Duke says, once I've hung up. He's still busily shooting the mess from innumerable angles. "Are you going to tell him what we did?"

"God, no." I can't believe these guys. "You obviously don't know him."

Back in the office, Henry is studying George. Of course, it's not really George, or the chances of it being him are extremely remote. I don't want to know what George looks like, especially after our few conversations. As far as I'm concerned, George looks like the boy in these JPEGs. I found them in a pedophile newsgroup. For all I know, they could be shots from some family vacation. For all I know, they could have been taken before I was born. For all I know, the boy in these pictures is dead. That would explain a lot.

Cycle

I remember being
17, loving myself.
It was such a shock
to turn 18 and feel
the tail end of my

parents' love, the
lack of a public's,
the offer of George's,
when it was too deep
for my purposes.

I love my characters.
They resemble George
slightly, though cuter
and less fascinating.
People say they're

sympathetic, that I'm
an evil genius. My

novel's more real
than the lives of its
readers, apparently;

does this mean I'm
loved again at 24?
I say, I'm on my way
there at least, with
or without George.

I get sick of fiction.
I'll be sick of George
too, I'm sure, but
never of myself. I
hate how that works.

NATETAN: Hi. Okay, so I read your e-mail, and opened
the pict file. You got my attention. What do you want?
ANONBOY16:   Want to know about George Miles.
ANONBOY16:   Hello?
NATETAN: Sorry. It's just a little weird.
ANONBOY16:   Don't know anything about him. Just know
you're connected to him.
NATETAN: Weird. Yeah, I am. So what do you want to
know?
ANONBOY16:   Everything. First, is he dead? Was told he was
dead.
NATETAN: Is he dead? Yeah, definitely. He killed himself.

ANONBOY16:   Sorry. Why did he do it?

NATETAN: Why? How do I know? It's a horrible world. I'm horrible. Everyone's horrible. Who knows what anything means? Why do you care?

ANONBOY16:   Kind of embarrassed to say. Think I look a lot like him. Guess that's part of the reason.

NATETAN: You look like me.

ANONBOY16:   Maybe I could come visit you. Research George's life and things like that. Think I might have lived there before, and . . . What do you mean I look like you?

NATETAN: You don't want to come here. It's a horrible place. Everyone here is either evil or they have evil things done to them. It's better not to know anything. I mean it. If you lived here before and got away, stay away.

ANONBOY16:   What did you mean I look like you?

How does it feel in the ground, George?
Cold and good, I guess. Feels right.
And you just lie there . . . and . . . ?
For a while now, enjoying the nothing.

And when the time moves along?
I'm just floating away to wherever.
You aren't afraid of the nothing?
What, of the worms and shit? No.

People say death is the ultimate.
So I've heard. Not my decision.

People say life is the ultimate.
It might be. I don't remember.

So why not just . . . kill myself?
That's a hard one to answer.
'Cos I'm tired of life's bullshit.
Well, there's no bullshit here.

So you'd recommend dying?
Hard to say. Why are you asking?
'Cos death seems so awesome.
Maybe, but all I ever feel is . . .

ANONBOY16:   So who was George Miles? Just curious. Know
there's something there.
NATETAN: Where do I start? My boyfriend Walker wrote
this amazing book about him. It makes George sound like the
cutest, most fascinating guy in the world, but then he supposedly flipped out or something. It's kind of mysterious.
ANONBOY16:   Strange. Why did he flip out?
NATETAN: I don't know. Too many drugs, I guess. There
was more to it than that, though. If you want to know my take
on the whole thing, I get the feeling that something horrible
happened to him. I think somebody raped and tortured him
and shit, and then nobody would sleep with him anymore,
and he couldn't deal with the loneliness. There are all these
hints about that.

NATETAN: Look, I'm lying. I can't tell you the truth. I
promised someone I wouldn't. I wish I could.
ANONBOY16:   Strange. That's what happened to me. A forest ranger found me in the woods about six months ago. Doc-
tors said I was raped and beaten and strangled. They say it's
strange I survived. Don't like to think about it. But that's
strange about George. Knew there was something.
ANONBOY16:   What do you mean you're lying?
NATETAN: I'm lying because . . . that's not the whole story.
ANONBOY16:   You won't tell me?
NATETAN: I don't trust the Internet. There are too many
people who spy on other people.
ANONBOY16:   Tell me a little. Please.

                    It's great you lived
                    at all, though maybe
                    not toward the end.
                    I loved your weird
                    mind, your easy
                    going face, deep
                    eyes, your long hair,
                    how it swished on
                    your shoulders, your
                    skin as tight as a
                    tree's, though your
                    life was shorter and
                    more exciting than

its. When you were
here, I thought only
of you, and went to
bed with any boy
who resembled you,
I was so haunted. So
I forgot who you were,
and you wanted me
to know. You're the
one who fired a gun
at his head, so high
on whatever, and so
depressed by my lack
of whatever that you
were afraid you might
otherwise not hit
the target, wherever
I was at the time. Not
with you, I guess. It's
finally hitting me now.

ANONBOY16:   Stop for a minute. That's a lot to take in, and
my mind's not so great. Let's chat about something else. But
it's good to know you're George Miles. Kind of figured you
were.
NATETAN: That's not even a third of the story. I didn't
even tell you about the time Walker made a film of me pre-

tending to shoot myself. That's when everything went sort of weird between us. Because it didn't mean enough to him, or some bullshit.

ANONBOY16: Let's be simple for a while. Do you mind? What are you doing right now?

NATETAN: Nothing. I'm just sitting around trying not to blow my brains out. Kidding. Or half kidding anyway. Like I said, that guy in my mirror is really pressuring me. Sometimes I think death would be the answer to everything. Have you ever heard of this band called The Omen?

ANONBOY16: No, don't know them. Sorry you feel bad.

NATETAN: They have this great quote about that. Shit, I can't remember how it goes. Forget it. So what are you doing?

ANONBOY16: Not much. Can't hear or talk, 'cos of what happened, I guess. Just stay by myself a lot. Take walks. Stuff like that. It's strange. Got some ideas and opinions, but I can't remember why I have them. So they're worthless. So I just watch people, and look around, and take notes. Thinking if I can figure others out, then I'll know who I'm not.

NATETAN: Wait, what are you talking about?

ANONBOY16: The forest ranger's been asking if anyone knows me. But so far nobody does. Starting to give up. George Miles is my only hope.

NATETAN: You're ignoring me.

ANONBOY16: Don't even know how old I am.

NATETAN: And you live in my mirror, right?

ANONBOY16: What?

ANONBOY16: Hello?

NAtetan: You know what I mean. Cut the shit, Walker.
It's you isn't it? You're so mean.
Anonboy16:   Don't understand.

> Your love held it
> in, or vice versa. I
> can't tell now, I'm
> so turned around.
>
> Things can't hold
> things. It's inap-
> propriate, I guess,
> feeling you here.
>
> If you're here, I'm
> more myself, I think.
> It feels real, but I'm
> alone in believing
>
> it's you. You don't
> feel it when I do,
> since you're not me,
> though I hold you so
>
> dear, so deep, past
> the point of knowing
> what's real. There's
> something there, but

it's not here. Here's
my thing, a thing
where you're held
all the time, or so it

feels. You shouldn't
have left me alone,
as I said. It makes
you too much of a

thing. Your thing
isn't love. It's here,
but that's mine, not
you. You're there.

NATETAN: Okay, I just opened that website. What the
fuck is going on? Those are pictures of me. What kind of bullshit is this? Who are you?
ANONBOY16:   Course they're pictures of you. What do you
mean?
ANONBOY16:   Hello?
ANONBOY16:   You still there?
NATETAN: You made the whole thing up, didn't you? How
do I know you're not lying? How do I know you're not some
friend of Walker's who's trying to fuck with my head?
ANONBOY16:   Don't know any Walker. Don't even know
how to lie.
ANONBOY16:   Hello?

NATETAN: You send me a picture that you say is you, but how do I know that? You say you wrote me because some psychic told you I'm George Miles's energy source or whatever, and now there's a website with all these pictures of me, and it says they're George Miles, and my dream in life is to be like him. It's pretty weird, even for my life.

ANONBOY16:   What are you saying? You're not George Miles? Don't understand, sorry. Don't know what's weird or not. My whole life's strange now. But everything I said is true.

ANONBOY16:   Hello?

NATETAN: Prove it. I want to come meet you. I really need to get out of here. Everything's fucked up with Walker. He doesn't believe in me anymore. What's your address and all that?

ANONBOY16:   Don't know. Live with that forest ranger in a tree house. It's miles from anything.

NATETAN: Right. Come on, please. Okay, I'm not George Miles. That was bullshit. I was just fucking with you. But you wanted to know about the guy in the pictures, right? That's me.

ANONBOY16:   Don't know what to believe. Don't trust you. You said you're a liar. You say you're not George. Then you say you are. Then you say those are pictures of you, but you're not George. Don't know what weird is, but that's weird.

NATETAN: I swear it's true.

ANONBOY16:   You swear what's true?

NATETAN: We can be friends.

ANONBOY16:   Friends how? You're a liar, and I don't know
who I am.
NATETAN: I know. It's perfect.
ANONBOY16:   No.
NATETAN: Please.
NATETAN: Tell me where you live. I'll hitchhike. No
problem.
ANONBOY16:   No. Gotta go.
NATETAN: Fuck.

I can't stumble backwards.
Not even a daydream
will light my way there.

Its history is historical.
Its point's been forgotten
and I grow inconsolable

when I think about then,
then so numb to everything else
I beg myself to reopen.

To spend one afternoon
like I did when George lived,
his beauty astonishing me,

my interest frightening him,
being too far from home.
His words few and slurred,

my words influencing no one.
I see straight through me.
I don't know how he felt.

I'm still his inattentive admirer.
There is someone that wild
about him still alive looking

over my shoulder at such
an illusion of him—a boy
I would kill myself to see.

—Walker Crane

Converse

The Omen's rustic van turned down a battered dirt road, into woods made unreal by a low, swishy fog. Etan saw a dim ghost off their one, crooked headlight, and stuck out his thumb. He had long hair, girlish cheekbones, no build, and a t-shirt inscribed with The Omen. He climbed in back, recognized their distinctive facades, and tried everything to impress them. Then Henry handcuffed and gagged him at knifepoint. When the trees nailed Duke's image of nowhere, he parked on a shoulder. They hustled the hitchhiker into a field, lit a campfire, and let him run around squawking until he collapsed on the ground like an exhausted tornado.

5:37: Hot in here. Muggy.
5:38: Opened the window some.
5:40: Birds, wind. Fog a ways off.
5:41: Tops of trees.
5:42: Maybe a wild dog.

5:45: Yeah, it is.

5:46: It's eating something.

5:50: Bored.

5:51: Gonna check my e-mail.

5:53: Waiting for it.

5:53: Fingers crossed.

5:54: Just one from Etan.

5:55: Wondering if I should read it.

5:56: Thinking.

5:56: Subject: Answer me or else.

5:57: Shit.

5:58: Reading it.

6:01: He's gonna kill himself if I don't answer.

6:02: Closed it.

6:03: Deleted it.

6:05: Sad.

6:07: Thinking I should take a walk.

6:08: Might help.

6:09: Looking down the ladder.

6:10: Yes, no, yes, no.

6:11: Climbing.

— Let me make sure this is working. Say something, Henry.

— Satan rules?

— Duke speaking. Hello, hello. Okay, I'm set.

— We don't have a ton of time. Not to mention it's freezing.

— I know. So what's about to happen?

— The whole story.

— Your call.

— From the beginning.

— Or not. Either way, let's get going.

— You mind?

— It's up to you.

— Well, we were on tour. During our vogue. You know all this.

— Forget me. I'm everyone.

— So . . . let's see, we'd just played the Hard Rock in Vegas, and I was in the casino—I forget where you were—and I saw this guy. And I thought, I want him. It was more than a thought. I had to have him. I was a little high. I thought, what do I want from him? I went down the list. Friendship, sex, boyfriend, mentor. Then I canceled them out for one reason.

— Being what?

— He wasn't into me.

— You could have said, I'm in The Omen.

— If I'd wanted to fuck him.

— And you didn't? Yeah, right. Back then? Come on.

— I wanted a quick, complete read. Sex, sure. Why not? But that wasn't the point. Sex was just the most obvious . . . whatever. This is strange.

— What's strange?

— Being interviewed as me. By you. I feel a little stiff.

— Stiff's okay. It's refreshing. So you thought, I want to kill him.

— No. No, I thought something like, I want to take him somewhere and find out what I want. It's just that before I saw him, I'd been confused. I'd think, Am I a sadist? I'm not. Am I a closeted murderer? No. I was categorizing, and when I saw him, I stopped.

— So why wasn't he your first?

— I don't know. Because I didn't know what I wanted. He was with friends. Plus, there was you. I didn't know what you'd think. I mean you you, not everyone you.

— I figured. What did he look like?

— You know. The obvious.

— Give me something concrete.

— Okay. Skinny, pale. Gawky. Turned up nose, long brown hair. You know, imagine my usual type without any Goth trappings.

— Hm. Lukas Haas in *Mars Attacks*? For the record.

— Less horsey.

— That guy in . . . the Bertolucci film. What's it called? Who fucks his mom? I guess that's a little obscure.

— Close. Maybe girlier. Let me think.

— Well, looking at him, and removing a few years, I'd say . . . the young Richard Lloyd. *Marquee Moon*, or just before.

— Wait. Vincent Kartheiser.

— In *Another Day in Paradise*?

— Younger. In *Heaven Sent*. No, wait, in *Masterminds*.

— I can see that. So do you regret losing out?

— What do you mean?

— That it was impossible with him.

— Well, it's not, as you know.

— I mean then. Don't be an asshole, Henry.

— No, no. It's perfect. If I'd murdered him then, he'd have just been the first. I've sort of blocked out the first one.

— The name escapes me. The guy who lived.

— Yeah, exactly. No, it's like fate. I just realize my whole "guiding their souls into Hell" overlay was the problem, and, bang, he reappears. I've practiced, I've learned, I've fucked up, and now I'm ready for him. Square one. Full circle. It's perfect.

— I guess we should say he's right here.

— Yeah. Over there. Five feet away. Less. Unbelievable.

— And you're absolutely sure it's him.

— I'm sure. He said so himself.

— Then as soon as you started to gag him, he said he'd been lying.

— He got scared. It's fucking obvious, okay?

— He also said he was immortal.

— Come on, Duke. It goes with the fan thing.

— So the first guy who says he was in Vegas that day is the one.

— It makes no sense, and it makes perfect sense.

— Maybe it makes too much sense.

— It makes everything up to this point make sense. To me, anyway.

— Look, what am I supposed to do here, Henry? Do I call you on this, or do I let you just play this thing out?

— You're upset.

— Bullshit. About what?

— About you-know-what. You're upset that it's over. That you're the less famous guy in The Omen again.

— I'm a lot of things.

6:31: Walking south, I think.
6:33: Can't tell.

6:35: Nicer trees. Smelling 'em.

6:38: More of 'em.

6:40: Feeling one's bark.

6:40: Colder than me.

6:41: Not as cold as the ground.

6:43: Strange leaves, too.

6:43: Reminding me of things.

6:45: One of 'em especially.

6:46: Important.

6:47: Tore it off.

6:47: It's in my pocket.

6:55: Just walked some more.

6:56: Wish I brung my coat.

7:01: Boulder or two.

7:03: Resting on one of 'em.

7:09: Something.

7:09: Over there?

7:10: Someone's coming.

7:10: Yeah.

7:10: A man.

7:11: Gonna hide behind the rocks.

7:13: Still hiding.

— So, indulge me, Henry. I want to throw out some reasons why people don't kill, and see what you say.

— You wrote them down? Let me see.

— Yeah, I have a list here.

— Wow.

— Quit looking. First, guilt.

— You're serious. Well, hunh. Okay, to feel guilt, I'd have to know that I fucked someone up. How can I know that? I can't possibly know what some dead guy's friends or family feel, since I don't know them. Let me guess. They cry, they're shocked, they're depressed, they're pissed off. Even there, I'm imagining things.

— Haven't you wondered what they'd have become? The guys.

— The world's here. It's doing fine. Nothing important is missing. Just little things, personal things.

— I still say you can't know that.

— What do you think would be different if they were around?

— The point is, you can't predict with teenagers. They're still developing. They're just human transitions.

— Exactly. They'd been some kid, but they weren't anymore. They might have become some adult. They were just these in-between creatures who lived to get high, and fuck, and listen to us, and whatever else. Make plans. So they had huge plans or goals, none of which would have panned. Remember us at nineteen? The Rolling Stones of the nineties? Ring a bell?

— You're generalizing.

— Sure.

— Then get specific. Pick one guy.

— Any guy? How about this one. To be boring.

— Him, right. He could do something three hours from now that he won't get to do.

— Okay, fine. What do we know about him? He's some hick.

He likes our stuff. He's into Satan. He was in Vegas once. Not that smart. Isn't artistic. Needs a bath. Pretty typical.

— And he's cute.

— He's cute. So he would have turned people on. Or been loved, had kids. Played bass or drums in a bad local band. Even that's pushing it. So you tell me what's missing.

— It doesn't matter what I think. You never feel guilt.

— I don't see the point in making up some adult and then blaming myself that he never existed. That would be psychotic.

— I'm not sure if you want to explain this on tape, but he's the last guy you're . . . well, we're going to kill, right?

— Well, that's the idea. That's the hope. Oops.

— What?

— I think he heard. I mean the guy. Look at him. He must know. Struggle, struggle, struggle. Amazing.

— Why don't you take off the gag and find out?

— Yeah, right.

— So, are you satisfied?

— With what? Oh, not really. That's what I'm saying. I thought I'd be somewhere much heavier than I am. I thought I'd be more than the nth guy who killed cuter guys. Ah, youth. But there's never been a better record. Thanks to you.

— Do you know that for sure?

— Pretty sure.

— Anything close?

— Well, how can I know? I've read things. I've seen what's around. Nothing I've seen tops the stuff that you've shot.

— So what have you seen? For the record.

— Well, the Berdellia stuff, the complete Randy Kraft stuff. All those guys. Kearny, Bonin, Gacy—
— Gacy? I didn't know he kept records.
— Sporadically.
— Any shots of Robert Piest?
— The last one. The gymnast.
— Yeah.
— Why?
— When I was a kid, I had a thing for Robert Piest, or the fact that he'd been murdered because he was cute, or something.
— He was classy.
— But when I read the accounts, it was such a letdown. Nothing happened. The guy wouldn't put out, so Gacy strangled him to death. It took, like, five minutes.
— Yeah, but for a moron like Gacy, who'd kill the first loser he saw on the street . . . to score with someone like Piest, a real teenaged boy with a promising life, then to throw that away . . . Damn. I wonder if he knew.
— Knew what?
— He knew . . . had to know that he'd never score bigger than Piest. And that he could never kill Piest, and do the kid justice. That he didn't have the brains, or the time, or the equipment. I'll bet it killed him to throw Piest away. I'll bet he would have sold his soul to do it over again. I'll bet no one else in the world even mattered to him after that. I'll bet he was completely in love.
— So were there any pictures?
— A couple. God, you're obsessed.
— They must have been "after" pictures.

— I'm trying to remember. I think he's lying in a bathtub. On his side, curled up. His pants are down around his knees. Maybe he's handcuffed, behind the back. Not great shots.
— This is embarrassing, but did he have a nice ass?
— A great ass. He was a gymnast.
— See, I don't know why, but I find that so frustrating.

7:31: He just left.
7:31: Hunter maybe. Had a gun and all.
7:33: Says a town's not too far that way.
7:33: East, I think.
7:35: Thinking.
7:36: Calculating when it'll be dark from the shadows.
7:37: Gonna walk there.
7:40: Dog. Looking strangely at me.
7:41: It's following me.
7:43: It stopped.
7:44: Just nicer and nicer trees.
7:49: Okay.
7:49: Looking down into a valley.
7:50: See buildings.
7:51: Simple ones, wooden. Some of 'em smoking.
7:53: Like whatchacallit.
7:54: Can't remember.
7:54: Hate myself sometimes.
7:57: Sorry. Sad.
7:58: Going down there. Got a feeling.
8:00: No trail anymore. Making one up.
8:04: Scared.

8:06: Just fell.
8:07: Skidded and ripped my pants.
8:07: Bleeding.
8:09: Can't walk too well.
8:10: Stupid, stupid, stupid.
8:16: House.
8:17: Can't walk anymore.
8:21: Crawling to it.

— I want to get back to the list.
— You mean away from Robert Piest.
— Yeah, so?
— I'm just making the distinction.
— So what about the spiritual stuff around murdering someone? You know, karma, the Christian Hell, blah blah blah.
— I'm one of those guys who thinks . . . what, religion's how wimps get their emotional exercise? I don't know, Satan rules? It's kind of a joke, all that. Religion. It's just like a tone, isn't it? Sometimes I half believe in fate, which is sort of spiritual.
— Fate as in . . .
— I don't know. That things happen. That time's sort of pre-arranged, maybe. We can't tell, because it's an avant-garde thing. A Walker Crane kind of thing. So we're part of it. When we're born, there's this weird, ordained path to our deaths. Our own little story line, maybe. And we take it. Is that too convenient?
— How would that work? I mean, who or what would have written it?

— Who cares? I don't know. It could explain all this. That's all I'm thinking. Anyway, I want to ask you a question.

— Me?

— A hypothetical. For my own curiosity. Let's say you could go backwards in time, and end up in Gacy's house on the Piest night. You have a gun, let's say. Gacy's getting the guy drunk or stoned or whatever he did. Drunk, I think. You know the guy's about to be killed. So you could do what you've done, and shoot pictures of Gacy's last stand, and give that gift to the world. Or you could kill Gacy, and save the guy's life. Or you could tie Gacy up, have your way with the guy, kill him, then untie Gacy and disappear into the future again, letting him take the rap. What do you do?

— That's hard.

— Why?

— Because my Robert Piest thing was based on two grainy headshots. If I was there, who knows? He might not work in person. And if he didn't turn me on, I might just feel pity or outrage or something.

— Trust me. From what I saw, he was your type. Even dead, I could tell.

— I don't know.

— Look, you know what the world's like without him. You don't know what the world would be like if he'd lived. You've experienced the future. You know his death's a little blip. You kill him, then return here without any guilt whatsoever. History hasn't changed. But you've fixed what you thought was a wrong.

— Look, I can say, Sure, I'd kill him. But if I was there, I don't know what I'd do. I'd probably take a few rolls of pictures.

— I was just curious.

— It's an interesting question. You'd kill him, obviously.

— If he happened to be on my way. No offense, but he had a weird jaw.

— Who, then? First stop–wise.

— I don't know. I think I'm more into the genie idea. Something less fixed.

— So make a wish. Or is it three?

— One's fine. That's easy. I want to go back to that night in Las Vegas.

— Use the time machine.

— Wait. So I stalk what's-his-name here.

— Etan.

— What?

— I think that's his name.

— So Etan walks around the casino, goes into the arcade, plays House of the Dead for an hour, and leaves. Now, here's the wish part. Let's say he dropped his room key. I wait for a while, until I'm sure he's asleep, and let myself in. It's dark, and I'm incredibly excited. You've never seen me that excited. I can't remember what it was like to feel that excited. Anyway, I walk in, and I can see him on the bed. Passed out, I'm thinking. I'm going nuts. I don't know what I want, apart from him. I have no idea. So I can barely walk, but I'm walking toward him, and then I see the blood. Then I see there's a gun in his hand. He shot himself. Like hours before. He's cold. He has rigor mortis. He's already lost the whole thing I was into initially.

— Suicide note?

— I used to imagine there was. And it said something like, I can't live with these fantasies of wanting someone to kill me.

But that's a little too Omen-esque. It's better if there's noth-
ing. No clues.
— Naked.
— No, not even that. I don't even get that. He's taken everything away.
— So you're not just redoing that videotape. You know, with
the cute guy.
— Hopefully, I am, but a baby step further. I don't get to see
my guy's body. I don't get sex. I don't get to be there. That's
different. That's a little better.
— So what do you do? Resurrect him?
— No, no. I've got excellent taste, but I can't take that chance.
What if he's . . . I don't know, a Deadhead? What if . . .
who knows? No, I know what I'd do. I'd kill myself. Right
then. Take his gun and do it. I'd feel what I felt, and then
end it.
— Seriously.
— Yeah. I think I would. Of course, that's easy to say.
— So, you're not going to shoot yourself now? I mean after
this deal? Please say no.
— I wish. No, I just change the beginning. That's all. Right the
wrong, like I was saying to you. It sounds contrived, I know.
But that's words. They're the problem. Words have this awful,
downsizing effect on your thoughts. Because to me, it sounds
profound. Shit.
— Yeah, except . . .
— What? Shit, now I'm depressed.
— Except how could it be him, Henry? I'm sorry. He wanted
us to fuck him, so he lied. That's the only difference between

him and them. Even I can barely tell them apart. Sometimes
when I'm labeling the pictures, I have to guess. The back-
grounds change, but the guys are identical. Same long hair,
same big lips, same turned up nose, same skinny body, same—
— I know. But I don't want to talk about that. In fact, let's just
stop talking altogether.
— So you do know.
— Off the record?
— Cross my heart. Look. Cross, cross.
— Yeah, I know. But you're the one who said it doesn't mat-
ter what I know. You're the one who said it's about how it
looks. So as long as you say it's him, and that my reaction's
the most profound, indescribable thing you've ever seen in
your life, then we're square.
— We're square. I mean . . . well, you know what I mean.
— Then let's do it. God, this is pathetic.
— Give me a second.
— We should never have talked. You ready?
— I guess.
— God, that was incredibly stupid.
— Wait. You're just going to shoot him? Wait a second.
— Yeah. Get ready.
— That's it?
— Yeah. Shut up.
— Okay, but—
— Shut up. Damn it. What's his name again?
— I told you. Etan. Or Eban, Eden . . . something like that. But
Henry—
— Hey, Eden.

8:28: Inside that house resting.

8:30: Really dark. Can't see.

8:34: My eyes won't adjust to it.

8:34: Wait.

8:35: Something different from the rest, but not much.

8:36: Stood up.

8:38: Tried to walk but it hurt.

8:39: Rubbing my leg.

8:40: Gonna try again.

8:41: Got two steps, maybe.

8:43: Lying here.

8:45: Shit.

8:46: Crawling.

8:50: Don't understand.

8:55: Still don't.

9:01: Like a maze.

9:03: Left, right, right, right, left, right.

9:05: Forget it.

9:08: Just been crawling.

9:09: Can't believe this.

9:10: Lighter ahead. For sure.

9:13: Please.

9:16: Almost there.

Curtains

Etan's sort of asleep by the scribbly dirt road. He's been out here for days, smelling rank when the sky's blue, and very bunched up when it's starred and cold. How can he possibly know shit? That's the lame-ass conclusion he's reached, drawn by eerily dumb, revolving thoughts. Everything's just a result of the sun gradually eating the earth, he guesses. Even that idea's too rigorous for his brain. He's nothing much, a small-town boy overly stuck in his head, which tends to refine one fantasy about The Omen and him, 'cos they're the only tape he owns. As far as he's concerned, they've driven down this exact road, picked him up, murdered him so many times that the picture's worn down to what's just so painfully personal to him. He can't come anymore. He's all raw. The batteries died in his boombox. Now it's him and the world again. He can't ignore the fact, seeing as how it's so gigantically around him. Not just the shit he can see. He means the world down this road, past those far off, unclimbable, fogged-over mountains. A place where folks merely exist, he figures. Like the trees, bushes, grass, et cetera, growing unevenly on either side

of his head. Maybe they'd move around more, but less mean-
ingfully than the stupidest animal he's ever seen in the woods,
even ants. That's ideal. Not wanting anything, even to eat food
or shit it back out. No one would care how they look, much
less how any other guys look. No one would want to screw,
love, or kill Etan, nor would he want to do that to anyone else.
There'd just be him, and a shack, and his stuff, and everything
would be able to talk, and every sentence would trigger ap-
propriate words in return, that's all. Like in some cartoon he
saw. So his shirt would be as cool as his friends. It could fas-
cinate him, or else he wouldn't give a shit if it was boring. If
it just talked about what it was made from, or how weird it
felt to be faded or ripped. Everything would have the same
consciousness, and pretty close to the same flat voice. No in-
dividual minds, no hearts, no instinctual shit, just movements
and ideas that fit in a pattern too simple to notice. Maybe that
pattern would be the thing folks call peace, if anyone ever
thought about peace, which they wouldn't. That's a pathetic
thought, he's very well aware. He just needs to eat. Anyway,
he wouldn't care about Noel. That's all. He wouldn't have
cried last night, wondering what Noel was thinking at that
millisecond, or how Noel might feel in his arms, or if Noel was
okay. There's a point where he can't know, unless he finds out.
Meaning grabs the dead boombox, stands, walks back home,
sees the real Noel, and asks. And even then.

Noel lies in the slanted rectangle of light tossed away by a
high, square, barred window. It spotlights his hand, pencil,

white sheet of paper, leaking far enough into the cell to put this glow on the page. He's drawing a picture of Dagger. Too bad he's untalented, 'cos he can't manage a likeness. Just messy lines trying to add up to something important, in his mind. Anyway, done. Or . . . wait, maybe he'll add a guy, him, standing there with his arm around Dagger, looking into those badly drawn eyes with a worshipful look, not that Noel's hand can simulate that kind of feeling. No, forget it. He crumples the paper.

Noel lies unbelievably motionless under the window. Its daylight feels warmer than anything anyone's touch ever gave him before, to think of life logically. Dagger is scattered in there, or has to be, or Noel imagines him there, which is the one thing that counts. Maybe the sun's an incompetent artist like him, who drew the world in hopes of replicating some idea a million times better. Maybe Noel and Dagger were drawn on the earth in hopes of nailing some love too profound to exist outside a mind so far away or psychotic. Maybe Noel is a sketch of someone he doesn't start to resemble, being too crude relative to the sun's imagination. Maybe . . .

There was a clearing, just past this slight crease in the woods where two deformed, leafless oaks twisted into a skull, if the sun and one's drugs were in gear. Etan was there, leaning back on the huskiest post that sort of held up Bob's awning, wacked on two faint sniffs of crystal.

Seeing a flash in the skull's deep-set eyes, Etan refocused his own. They held out the usual hope for whatever. Hey, he said, decoding Bob. Long time. Luckily, there was a rasp to his voice, so he came off bored. But it was just some dust left in his throat from those days by the road.

I knew you'd be here, Bob said. He threw away his ax, slid his less calloused hand down Etan's jeans, and recaptured that flat as Hell ass. So it wasn't a pillow stuffed with a cathedral, as his thoughts had solidified George's. Still, it formed this unusual pact with the past, or there was nothing else.

How do you know shit? Etan said. In advance and all that. Then Bob's fingertips cross-referenced Noel's. The mix-up created this crystal-tweaked ache in the mulch that attached Etan's face to his skull. It made him kiss Bob, which looked right, but felt unbelievably confusing.

10:07: Dark.

10:07: Keep writing that.

10:07: Know it.

10:10: Been days now, I guess.

10:17: Nothing else.

10:32: Shit. Not again.

10:33: See my mind.

10:34: A white dot.

10:34: Really think so.

10:36: Enlarging.

10:41: Watching it.

10:42: Blossom.

10:46: God?
10:50: Can't describe it. Sorry.
10:51: Sorry.
10:54: Blinded by it.
10:55: Can't hardly see.
10:56: Can't see what I'm writing.
10:59: Scared.

— See? Him. Follow my flashlight.
— Hunh.
— Dagger. Real as me.
— Close, but . . . Nah. Weird, though. Fuck, it's cold in here.
— He's even writing in a notebook.
— Dagger's dead, Etan. Thanks to you.
— Yeah, so why aren't you still back in jail? Think about it.
— 'Cos the sheriff's an idiot?
— Whatever. So, I was thinking. We traded with Satan, right?
That's why I'm immortal, and got to hang with The Omen.
That's why you supposedly got your big, secret thing you
won't tell me about.
— You hung with The Omen. Right.
— Okay, maybe not. I still say that's him.
— But if that's Dagger, then Satan didn't get shit, so he wouldn't
have given me shit in return.
— Maybe Satan gave you a freebie. 'Cos you're cool.
— I was there, man.
— Maybe Satan threw him back.
— Dagger was a gazillion times cuter than this guy.

— I guess. But he's sort of scarred up, so who knows?

— Anyway, Dagger looked like you. If anything, this freak looks sort of weirdly like me.

— You think?

— What, you don't?

— Maybe. Okay, I see what you're saying. Hunh. He's not bad.

— So that's not Dagger, is it? Asshole.

— If you say so, asshole.

— Then I've seen enough.

I need your help, Etan yelled, and grabbed ahold of the strange, Noel-like guy, so he wouldn't limp off. There were some jiggles and creaks in the shack's saggy build, followed closely by Bob. "Noel" hid his eyes, being a scaredy-cat, or on account of the sky's wearing far too much sun.

Who's your friend? Bob said, shielding his eyes. They were total dead ends, in Etan's thinking. So it was chilling to see them so warm, like they'd just been redrawn by some Disney-ish thought. He entered the unkempt front yard, just as "Noel" took a peek through two fingers. George?

You know this guy? Etan said. Then he stepped back and kicked around dust, while they hugged, and so forth. He couldn't relate, except to feel like it should either be him getting groped, or him groping some guy who looked more like a slightly trashed Noel every lame, passing second.

— Do the trees look different to you? Noel.

— What?

— Look over there. Them. See?

— It's summer. They're dead.

— Okay, maybe I mean everything's different. Like you. You seem . . . I don't know, cold.

— I guess. But you're the one who's acting all warm, man.

— Less weird, you mean.

— No, that's not what I mean. I mean . . . Okay, wait, let me study you for a second. Look at me. Don't blink.

— What?

— Give me a sec. I have to get Dagger's face out of your face. 'Cos you're not quite as awesome as him by these fractions of inches, and stuff. No offense. Hold still. And stop crying.

— Fuck.

— What's your problem?

— I don't know. The look in your eyes isn't something enough.

— See? This is what I'm saying, Etan. You're a fucking mess. I just told you. I asked Satan to make me immune to you. It's too late. Give it up.

— I'm sorry. It's just . . . I feel a lot for . . . shit. For you.

— You've gotten totally weird. Or else I can see you better now that I don't give a shit. Yeah, that's it. Interesting.

— No, but I always felt this. I just couldn't . . . tell. I didn't know.

— You're pissing me off.

— It's that fucking Dagger guy. You only like him 'cos he's dead. Or 'cos you want him to be dead, or I don't know. Wait.

— You're embarrassing yourself, man.

— Wait.

3:18: Tell me what I was like.

3:18: Excited.

3:19: His lips said, Like you are now.

3:19: Don't understand.

3:20: His lips said, Look at yourself in the pond, George.

3:20: Leaning over to see.

3:21: Waiting on some ripples.

3:23: Still don't understand.

3:23: His lips said, Aren't you amazing?

3:24: Guess so.

3:24: What about inside?

3:24: His lips said, You tell me.

3:26: Trying to see.

3:26: His lips said, Try your eyes.

3:27: Checking 'em.

3:28: Look confused, I guess.

3:28: Help me.

3:30: He's thinking.

3:32: His lips said, Let me look.

3:34: Both of us looking at me in the pond.

3:45: His hand's on me.

3:47: It's rubbing.

3:47: His lips said, Look now.

3:48: I look scared.

3:51: Scared.

Etan dragged a broken chair to the table, and sat. He stuck a fork in his portion of rabbit, and smeared a crude Satan face

on the plate. Bob and that George or whoever were set-
tled down, saying grace or some insanity. So, listen, Etan
mumbled. Would you care if I screwed your friend?

Don't even ask, Bob mumbled. The shack was deserted,
apart from the obvious shit, plus these ashen, rectangular
planes where Bob's art had deprived walls of daylight for
fucking ever. The culprits were smoky, black sticks in the
roaring fireplace. 'Cos the answer is, Not on your life.

Come on, Etan said, and took a huge, ugly bite. It had
this forgettable, millionth-time taste. Still, he tried to get into
its being some innocent thing from the woods. But the taste
wasn't evil enough to supplant what his damaged mind's
dilated eye had been foreseeing for weeks. You can watch?

Etan jacks off in his secret campsite, helped along by The
Omen on boombox. He's a tensed scrawl, as usual, beating
the shit out of his worthless crotch. He can't get that George
creature out of his mind, noise or not. A wild dog trots sud-
denly out of some nearby bushes in its mechanical way, hop-
ing Etan's not around, so it can raid his shit. Its ears pick up
on the music, which sounds like the weirdest fight between
the most unusual animals it's ever heard. So it cautiously
scampers up onto one of the boulders that gives it an aerial
view of the porn. It can't figure Etan out, being a simple con-
struction. It sees shapes and a motion, and smells the inter-
national odor for crotch, which rivets it to the view, though it
can't figure out how to use the excitement it feels. It's never
bored, just hypnotized, which is a glorious thing, or would be,

if Etan realized it was there, and understood how it thought, and could learn anything that wasn't hidden away inside loud, creepy songs. So when he opens his eyes for a second, and sees the dog, life's predictable. He grabs a gun from his belongings, and shoots. It falls dead by his side. He's so fucked up. It was so stupid.

— Satan, it's Etan. I don't know where Noel went. He flaked. He's fucking lost it. I don't think he's into you anymore. I'm sorry. But I just need to talk. You don't need to do anything heavy.
— Whoosh, rustle.
— Can't you talk? I can't believe that's not one of your deals. It can't be that tricky.
— Whoosh, chirp, chirp, rustle.
— Oh, right, wait. I forgot. Here, let me . . . press Play.
— Click, whirr.
— Okay, I call to you, Satan. I can't fucking deal with this world anymore. It's so intense right now. I don't know if it's me, or Noel, or that George guy, or Bob, or everything.
— It's black, black, black, black, black, black.
— Come on, please. I'm so fucked up. I really need you. Look, I killed a dog and everything. It's yours. Take it.
— It's black, black, black, black, black, black.
— Weird. That's you, isn't it? I mean what The Omen is singing. 'Cos those aren't the usual words, I'm pretty sure. Well, I'm not completely sure. I don't know this song as well as some of their others. Okay, is this you?

— We're black, black, black, black, black, black.

— Right. Whoa. Good, good. Listen. Will you do me a huge favor? Obviously, I'll pay you back.

— We're everything you've dreamed, you've dreamed.

— Can you reverse time? I want to go back to how it was before Noel and me asked you to give him that Dagger freak. Except I'll be the only one who remembers what happened since then. So, that. That's what I want. What do you say?

— Black merges with black, black merges with black.

— Meaning what, man?

— We're gonna turn you so black, black, black, black.

— Are you going to do it or not? No offense.

— Death is so black, black, black, black, black, black.

— What are you fucking saying?

— You're gonna die, die, die, die, die, die.

— Go ahead.

— We'll help you die, die, die, die, die, die.

— Totally. Go ahead.

Etan spied Noel by the decrepit, rank creek bed. He crouched, made a scruffy decision, then clutched at Noel's jeans, balls, dick, and maybe pubes, in that order. Sure enough, they went rorschach.

Noel kicked Etan's shin. Then he gathered his pencils and pad, and took off in the direction of home, cursing everyone's emotions but his own. To get there, he had to pass through that acre-square place only they'd recognized, which was fucking unfortunate.

Etan caught up with Noel, despite the new limp.

Maybe the place had some vibe, strange. Maybe things fell together a certain way, either by artistry, or by nature's vast accident, and worked the feelings of simpler folk, say these guys. Or that explained why Noel hugged Etan back. Or it was boredom, or guilt.

Etan stripped. He possessed Dagger's pale, meatless body, or almost. But his face messed so hard with the original, Noel had to open his sketchpad, and prop it nearby to stay hard and all that.

Noel stripped. He was so unbelievably cute, on the surface at least. No one in town should have been that important to Etan. It killed him.

7:11: He's screwing me. Hard to write.

7:14: Tried to look back at him.

7:18: Gonna try again.

7:19: Not sure what I saw.

7:22: Had to bite my hand for a minute.

7:26: Excuse me.

7:26: You said something.

7:26: His lips said, No, I didn't.

7:32: Biting my hand again.

7:38: He rolled me over.

7:39: Worse like this.

7:41: He put his face before mine.

7:42: Looking at me.

7:48: Shut my eyes for a while.

8:48: He's still looking.

8:52: His lips said, I can't believe it.

8:57: Bit my hand.

9:03: He looks confused.

9:05: Worse pain.

9:07: Hard to write.

9:08: Can't think.

9:08: His lips said, I don't believe it.

9:10: He shut his eyes.

9:13: Thinking.

9:14: Might write, I love you.

9:16: Waiting 'til he opens his eyes.

9:18: Waiting.

9:20: He hit me.

9:21: Not sure if I feel it now.

9:22: He hit me again.

9:23: More.

9:24: Gonna shut my eyes.

Bob and Etan traipsed miles up the steep, fading trail. Then Bob carried him most of the last stretch, 'cos he was exhausted. When they reached the plateau, Bob's spooky "house" was this jagged black rug, airborne bits of which twirled between a gridwork of flames and some current.

Etan warmed, then Bob told him this story. About Dagger, and George, and love, and a town just like theirs, except

even more backwards. There was some Satanic stuff, but the
love was confusing. So that screwed up the far better, creepi-
est parts, which was maybe Bob's point.

The fog built up, did its worthless magic. Etan lost Bob,
stumbled around, found the trail. When the embers went out,
Bob slipped a gun from his coat, and located his head. Back
in town, his death made this noise like when any guy killed
something out in the woods, so no one heard.

— I can't believe we're doing this. Brr.
— Light the candles. Be cool.
— Okay, but you owe me.
— Now kill the cat, and put it in the middle. You remember
the drill.
— You do it. It's your thing.
— Fine. Hand it over. There, there. Big fucking deal.
— Yuck. Keep that away from me.
— There. Now hit Play.
— This is so lame. I can't believe you're still into this shit. I
can't believe—
— Ssh. Satan, you there?
— I hate this song. Can I say that?
— Shut up. Satan, make yourself known. Do your thing. Do
something trippy like put out the candles, or screw Noel, or
something, so we'll know.
— Ow.
— Cool.
— I'm faking it, asshole.

— You know what, Noel? Things like that are why I'm doing this, if you care. You've gotten so complicated or something.
— Oh, wait. Shit. It's real now.
— Liar.
— Ow, ow. Ask what you're going to ask, for God's sake. Ow.
— Okay, okay. Satan, I want George as a sex slave. He'll want me. He'll . . . I'm sort of embarrassed to say it, but . . . love me, and . . .
— Hurry.
— He'll do anything I want, in bed and wherever else. So, that's it. And, you know, thanks in advance.
— Why does he always screw me?

2:03: Sitting here.
2:04: Bird. Red one. In that tree.
2:05: Two of 'em.
2:05: Sitting close together.
2:08: They're just looking at everything.
2:10: For enemies, I guess.
2:12: They're never sure.
2:13: Birds are one thing multiplied?
2:14: 'Cos of love?
2:16: One flew off. Can't see him.
2:16: Other one doesn't care.
2:18: Feel like shooting the other one.
2:19: Is this my thought?
2:20: Can't decide.
2:21: Hate myself sometimes.

2:23: It flew off.

2:25: Should have killed it.

2:26: Just looking around.

2:27: Those two guys again. By the creek.

2:28: One of 'em's looking at me.

2:28: He reminds me of someone.

2:29: Can't remember.

2:30: Wondering if I should wave.

2:30: Just did.

2:30: He waved back.

2:33: Bored.

"Just go talk to him." Noel shrugged. He was sitting cross-legged, head lowered, a few locks of flyaway hair in his eyes. Still, he liked the effect on his drawing. It was cribbing together a face out of some swirled, crushing memory that made its way through a dense feeling, possibly love. "What's your problem?"

"I will, I will." Etan swatted flimsily at a bee. It came rocketing off the pond, which stunk of things he didn't care one shit about. But he looked there, deeply into that mulch, and thought about death, so as not to seem too wild for Noel. "Give me a second."

"You're gonna blow it." Dagger's blank, graphic face edged fractionally from the loose web of lines, eyes first. They loved Noel for coercing them back, even if nobody else saw anything but some loose pencil marks. Still, the idea got Noel hard, as Etan saw. "Make your move."

"Okay." Etan studied Noel's crotch. It was way too mean-
ingful, being Noel's. So he concentrated on George, who was
nearly as cute, if nothing else. That, plus the crystal meth
lodged up his nostrils, got Etan hard. It wasn't perfect at all,
but nothing could be in this town. "Wish me luck."

A little town stuck far away in some obscure hills attached to
the rest of the world by a dirt road that swerves dangerously
through ugly trees and a fog so dense no one else thinks about
making the drive though occasionally strangers will come by
mistake and take a brief look around then realize how unim-
portant its buildings and residents and beliefs seem where-
upon they'll turn back not moved enough to tell anyone they'll
ever know for the rest of their lives that it crossed their cir-
cuitous minds once.